This Love

This Love

Z A Bukhari

PARTRIDGE
A Penguin Random House Company

To order additional copies of this book, contact
Toll Free 800 101 2657 (Singapore)
Toll Free 1 800 81 7340 (Malaysia)
orders.singapore@partridgepublishing.com

www.partridgepublishing.com/singapore

to my

Mother

with love

Contents

Chapter 1

It is always safe to stand for a particular person and seek for his appearance in a crowd, when his class line is allowed to the gates. Look for him just when the school time is over and all students are at rush to exit. Sara wants it secret un-noticed and there under the shade of the gates closer office she would stand for several weeks at school off timings. Other some girls would gather as to wait for their drivers or to clear away the crowd near the gates so she had another perfect reason to keep standing there, her wait for her driver would also continue providing her a solitary excitement of her life. She with a legal size note book covered in white lamination cuddling it almost and almost providing a cover to her face keeping the file vertically just under the eyes, eyes she needs to remain steady to sweep through the path way towards the gates. One thing she cannot assess or may be later in her life, when she would summarize this part of her life then maybe, she would be able to differentiate the thrill of waiting for him or the sparkling joy of having his sight. The school was an English medium one where except Urdu and Islamic studies rest of all the subjects were taught in English, yet doing O levels was an option students were also encouraged to speak English. There were two senior branches Boys branch and Girls branch. Inside the same building these two had separate structures and strict discipline was observed, so no girl or boy of senior section was allowed to talk to each other not even the male and female teachers were allowed except during the staff meeting within a well monitored environment. The announcement of O Levels boys section was made and there was a line of some fifteen elderly looking boys, unlike the instinctive assertions they were giving rather gentlemanly, yet stylish looks perhaps they all were at their lessons of heroes of Jane Austen novels, or perhaps they were conscious of being observed, whatever, but for one it was sure he was the second last of the fleet. As he appeared her breath really gets disturbed or the heart throbs more than the usual but this wasn't her study, such a study must be made by a mother of a growing daughter. The extra circulation of blood, making cheeks rosier, thus cuddling the same legal size file with a neutral white appearance she never knew how swift or slow the time passes while he the second last of the line walking towards the gates when moves out from the inner gates, toward the outer gates for that particular moment, she would always start looking at a younger girl a sister of a senior girl the younger was always trying to finish her lunch-box before facing her mom. Though it was not an appropriate sight to look at, while someone is eating but the courage she needs to keep looking at him approaching by six or seven steps, it was impossible for her. She cannot tell why with the passage of time she tries to avoid staring him. Earlier some weeks ago, it wasn't that tough or that much exiting experience only keep waiting, keep watching keep pursuing the watch and then enjoying the feel of having accomplished a task just that, but through and through the experience was getting into complexity. It is undefined why after a heart-charging wait she turns her sight, she hasn't stared in the eyes or it is his eyes she wanted to escape of not being caught by him, seeing him. Perhaps the same verbal structure of the sentence seizes her heart and she became over-shy. But not missing the last sight of his turned back, and exiting from inner gates. This she maintained with some missed opportunities but for last few days her timing was adjusted remarkably well coordinated. The whole procedure was something like waiting, announcement, marking the one from the end of the line (always there perhaps he was the fresh enrolment), staring only, when he is far away but with his nearing pace her eyes would go blink as to get ready to avoid and the final moment comes just before turning to the inner gates complete avoidance and then promptly looks there as to not miss the back view sometimes got a glimpse of side pose before disappearing through the inner gates it gave a bounty to her, feels so successful and filled.

He was not but she, was a fresh enrolled. It is been months since her family shifted in this area and her father got her enrolled before summer vacation with heavy donation as to allow her to complete her class 10th with board exam. She had done her 9th class with board exam from the school at place where they were living earlier the school was just two months new for her and he was newer than that. Thus benefited of being new, it was her third day at school when an unexpected rain happened just after the break, the sky grew darker the wind blew noisy; windows of the classrooms were instantly shut to avoid shatter mess but insiders, teachers and the taught both aspiring to enjoy the spectacular. Yes school was big and providing various landscapes of play-grounds, assembly grounds trees a deeper ground which was not allowed to be tread by any one because it was near the gates presenting the visitors a welcoming note so that particular deeper ground filled with rain water. There were clouds in the sky since morning but rain in September is rare. The rain had stopped just then it was the third day of her regular classes, a maid entered in the class slipping a paper slip in the fingers of the teacher to read, it was for Sara asking her to come to the senior headmistress of girls branch. She was made sent instantly as the orders were from that teacher's reporting officer. The same maid escorted her but by half the way the maid making a gesture to the right, she turned, asked her if she could go by herself. Going all alone, after a few steps on the same passage she had to make a stop a trail of very small kids aging two and half years was creeping slowly each child was holding the shoulders of the child ahead of one, thus making a long train and guarded by two very active good looking teachers all this platoon was the fresh enrolled Montessori class and their off time comes two hour earlier than the usual school off times. Nobody breaks the train as it creates havoc on the new innocent beings, this she did not know but she enjoyed, kept waiting and watching them go it was an unusual sight because in her previous school, a typical girls school an English medium one, where only English is taught in English the virtue of claiming it an

English medium was all lying on the fact that English was taught from the beginning, the Good morning was said in harmony in the morning and Good afternoon was rhymed in after break hours, students could ask in English if they want to go for drinking the water and for the washroom and maintenance of such hi fi Montessori was not kept there, a well ridden it was, forgetting that, she was amusing this small train as to add a new part in her observation about new school just then a moment dawned and she looked on her left to where the train was going it was a small arch shape gate an opening from girls branch to boys branch and this all train was going there to reach the main gates, escorted with their teachers, and there. just outside the arch there was him, he was also keenly watching the children and letting them go he was smiling he also twitched a healthy baby's dropping bubbly cheek, she assessed that she just enjoyed them going but he became a part of their slow fun train almost leaning, smiling and even saying something to them his eyes were smiling too, eyes do smile her first exploration, absorbed he in their fun had become a part of the scene. Just then the last baby of the train went and he went to his way but she could not go from this moment, she carried it, the train was gone and the scene was over so she went ahead to see the senior mistress. Is this called the first sight? So it was this.

Nothing started, no extra throb, no missed pulse waiting, watching, blushing there was no start to anything, that week went casual. She in the newly shifted home was slowly doing unpacking. Daily after school times her mother would ask her to see in the cartons and arrange things in her room the cartons were placed in her room by the maid in the morning. She, after school would take help of the maid in arranging cupboard, book shelf, wall hangings and the like. It took a fortnight to them to properly doing unpack and arrange things. just before the full furnishing the house and of course after the episode of the school kids train meaning after the episode of his first sight one evening her elder brother entered shouting and started yelling at her, his words were full of insult he was referring her to a very low example with the support of the fact that she is going into a co-education school, all he wanted was the sound-system from her room, she tried to maintain the plea that it is the maid who has placed it here she doesn't use it. he grabbed the system and kicking side table to make his way started to take the system to his room, she could not remain quiet she protested saying

"Papa bought you the computers thus leave this to me"

"Leave this to you so that you also get spoilt" a prompt stroke was returned

That evening processed into a night with dreams full of opened eyes. It wasn't difficult for her to reconcile with herself she was made habitual of such "also" citations and negative references. After finishing her homework, she started learning a test of Pakistan-studies. That night before sleep, when she was making sure of all work done putting the fallen side-table upright, just then the fiery blaze of two scorn full eyes filled tears in her eyes there was a question why, only by having complete resemblance why everyone thinks she will be exactly like the one, the one that missing one in the family. Just then while she was fighting with face fortunes and face faults many faces float through her film of imagination most of them were from her new school and there all of a sudden her imagination reel be stilled there was a face with sweet smile leaning graciously weaving and chatting also twitching one's cheek that smile that personality looked so benevolent full of good mood and friendly gestures. Was that the need of her shocked mind to re-cover by getting the benefit of some happy scene as the therapist do to post trauma patients, was her mind itself replacing that evening's grim picture with a good one to solace her to calm her to put her to sleep if this is true then love is our mind's technique, hearts are blamed without reason. No, not love, it did not start, but imagining this, him, really put her to sleep and the next day she was back to original. Such incidents go quicker or the sensitivity of the growing girl was functioning sharply or perhaps being a sister-less and a new to the new environment yes all reasons work together to enhance her solitude more, her mind supplied her with more sauce of imagination on already a spread of an image. She experienced more secure time segregated from others. It was her need, convinced, for doing perfect home work for getting A+ on weekly tests and staying ahead of the class she needed that, needed to imaging him, it is been three weeks since she first saw him, her imagination had improved in many episodes until then she had imagined him giving sweets and chocolates to the children and to her, her imagination gave more rich coloring to the arch shape small gate where she first saw him she decorated it with vines and flowers hanging exactly upon them. This vision had become a source of energy from mere a shock observer; everybody was surprised seeing her doing things perfect in a more competitive environment. Love; is it a drug? She did not know love, but she was taking the drug. That day when another girl of senior section asked her to come and sit in the chairs for the visitors, in a veranda of admission office building nearest to the inner-gates she surprisingly asked" is it allowed to us to sit here" a new remains new until one accommodates oneself. That another girl relaxingly stated "where should we go then! See it is a big crowd and it will take ten minutes more and when there are no visitors so we may sit" she was already sitting. But Sara chose not to sit, apologetically explained her driver must be there. It was this moment or the next but on the same occasion she got surprised another sight, she saw him again, she wasn't expecting, that means something, however it was a simple fact one who comes has to go and if the exit gates are the same so it is very probable to see a person in times more than the level of boredom but there grew excitement. Towards the whole evening until before sleep she kept on wondering that she saw him. Her thoughts were unfixed this time her imagination could not induce her to work; the drug of imagining him, all of a sudden became ineffective. It needed to pour something more into it. Instead of taking the simple fact that everybody who goes to school comes back, it is as natural, her mind who had already placed his position to some celestial being instead of letting her think a simple thing simply, putting her in the labyrinth of so many questions and so much curiosity. That night was a different one, who he is, which class he is in, what if she could see him again, and does he use the same passage to the gates many silly, o o, no, very important things came into her mind. She slept only with the conclusion that she had been silly relying on just once chanced appearance while there can be many, daily and all in her hand. Her sleep that night was not sound the next morning she had been in hurry, hurry of waiting, waiting for the off timing. It started then. No not love, the curiosity. With every single day the curiosity filled charm, the charm provoked fear; the fear enhances the taste of adventure. It is now peak of sensation when from inside out she would wait and watch. It is very recent that she developed hesitance of being seen, being caught. The other day her mother reminded her of the dress which the maid had put on a hanger in her cupboard, her mother told two things with equal importance that the dress she had bought from the boutique from the area's best mall, and tomorrow after school in the evening Sara has to go along with her to her aunt's (her mother's sister) house wearing that, "jimmy has come Pakistan on leave" she added. The cupboard which she was about to open to see her new dress, remained closed as she remember that she got to do preparation of two tests.

Chapter 2

It is also safe when one has approached to the appointed place well in time, and it gives comfort to see others are making haste to avoid getting late and this gives pleasure to find someone finishing a thing abruptly to make haste to reach at the appointed place. He, the well in time boy was Omer the second last of the O Levels line, standing towards the end of the line, was providing him a perfect opportunity to see the most hilarious scene of that moment. She was not running, nor was she slipped but she was entangled all in her hair and making a furious effort to tie them in a braid that it became quite a scene. A perfect composition of rush, her quickly knitting fingers, her unruly wet hair braid and her head movement back and forth seeing other girls already going down, but she in the middle of the stairs standing at one side. giving way to the other rushing down girls, was still receiving pushes and all her retaliation was observed on her hair with her fast knotting fingers but her hair was too proved dis-cooperative and this dis-cooperation prolonged as the hair was long and the passage downwards was long too and the line in which she was to stand was a long way away to the stairs so she did not prolong any longer, just leaving rest of the braid undone she spread *dupta* to cover her head in a manner to cover her unfinished braid from the back and went down through the stairs to join the morning assembly. The girls branch and boys branch assembly were also solemnized separately in their particular building blocks but a glimpse of girls could be caught through a narrow opening between a tree and the other building there were stairs and for some 6, 7 steps the stairs-users could be seen from the boys branch assembly ground. There was strict prohibition on keeping the hair loose opened when they are longer than the shoulder-touching. First this rule was imposed on school girls only, latter female teachers of senior section were also made to follow the rule. Each morning a strict monitoring was practiced with novelties of penalties and the rule became a tradition when last time the girls were sent home with their parent after a warning phone call from school to invite them to collect their fashion-babes back. Such news were known more to the boys branch as each branch admin always wants publicity to be ahead on the other in maintenance of stricter discipline. Now it was evident that one is new to school because one is new to the norms and it was her first or second day and not the third because on third there were clouds in the sky but that day it was sun and it glowed more gold on the stairs, after this moment that sun never set, it grew to its pinnacle, it glowed, it burned but it stayed there inside him forever. The recitation commenced, everybody quieted, assembly was over and the classes began as usual. A two three times that day he tried to share but he had made others, habitual of listening them. Once during the break time when they all were very tense at the surprise class of physics was about to be taken by senior headmaster of the boys branch (physics was his zone) just after the break. They all were in rush of learning abruptly (he the headmaster used to work with oral testimony at the spot to check student's ability and to assess teacher's hard work) thus holding books and note books they had their break time gone in front of them. In such tense moment Omer could not seek a perfect opportune to share what he saw in the morning the class seems so serious. After the surprise visit of the headmaster was over he tried to share while everybody was to comment on the hastiness in which they prepared for the test, the test went well and everybody was relieved he tried again to share by giving a start "people at the girl's branch are far too beyond understanding…" Sameer broke "their headmistress does not give such surprise test she is lenient I do not understand of our headmaster" "see we were asked to prepare for the term but he took test random", another added. "There are many things that go random in this school" perhaps this time he was about to target random hair discovery but Ayaz cut him "school is good, my elder brothers also have studied here"

Ayaz was friend and neighbor of Omer and Omer too has begun his schooling from the same. Standing always at the second last position in the line was funny because his class had to make a turn, from there they all had to make turnabout … interesting! Being first or being second last makes no difference to Omer for his house was on the same street just in front of the school. Omer doesn't remember, years ago, they moved from village and bought this house in this area. His sisters also did their schooling from the same school. (Earlier this area was not that commercialized but with the passage of time the land rate rose and now for the people, buying property here, it was quite a status for them.) That day he could tell this to nobody and at home the probability was narrowed as the members were remained few. His elder sisters have got married and settled with their husbands, now he, with his grandfather and mother, they all were very alone, his father died when he was 11 Upon coming home instead throwing bag and kicking out the shoes to the corners of the room he did all changing very carefully placing each thing to its right place. Instead of asking for food he went straight to the kitchen asking his mother, with a smile of an explorer if he might bring *roties* from the *tandoor* telling her that he has seen clothes been washed today and she must be very tired. The mother lovingly told that the maid does the washing and she just helps her and she is not tired and asked him to see if his grandfather has come from mosque, then they should serve the lunch. "We both came almost together the mosque is far while my school is near sometimes I wish it could be the otherwise" "We should always be thankful to Him son!" proposed grandfather he was entering in the TV lounge. They had their lunch and just according to routine he collected the used utensils and took them to the kitchen sink and washed them. Meanwhile his mother and grandfather went to their rooms for a short nap. He also went to his room it was infect a study; his father had arranged books with his hands. Not alone the books on law, other so many books of world's classic literature of different languages with translation were stacked very nicely his father was

a lawyer. He had high aspirations for his only son but
there he was with aspirations and him, his father no
more… sometimes by pursuing aspirations we mitigate
the melancholy of missing member. He would do dusting
and cleaning of this room himself, each year the progress
reports, the certificates on essay writing and other such
souvenirs he would place right under the pile of books, his
father wrote. A peculiar way to cherish ownership, his to
his father and his father's upon him. He still hasn't learnt
to share any pink of his life because he hasn't one. That
evening went casual, Ayaz, his neighbor and class mate
came, they both reminded each other of the term tests and
the grades required, grandfather too participated in their
discussion in an hour he went back bearing a message for
his mother from Omer's mother something like she will
pay visit to decide for the shopping together. The night
came with same activities mother cooked for the dinner
the three of them took together he cleared the table and
washed plates leaving big utensils for the maid, and finally
made tea for his grandfather after some twenty minutes it
was time to bed. Omer used to sleep in his grandfather's
room this was his mother's recommendation to make
him offer morning prayer in time and also to take care
of his aged grandfather but each night before going
to bed Omer would spent some time in the study and
sometimes nights, doing late night studies he would sleep
in the couch of study so this room was more in his use.
That night he went in the study to prepare for a test, he
did that with full usual concentration. The next few days
were similar routine days of school boy's life, home work,
and preparation of tests so in one similar night, here he
was again in the study learning paragraph by paragraph
by heart and assessing his work of learning in parts he

always used small note pad in which he would write the key words of the lesson and trick was simple in first time reading, he would allow him to look at the key words, each key word would provide him the start or content of that particular paragraph but next time he would place hand over them to assess his learning, even then sometimes he had to peep for a key word Only sometimes. During all that a lead pencil would stay in his right hand and during learning he would keep on drawing lines, dots circle into circle, leaves, hut, and trees around these key words. One could see that the outer line of an image he would draw without much care but the inner detailing used to be of much explained quality. It was simple by reading out to himself the rough sketch around a key word he drew and while revising he would keep shading in the image. This night the usage of note pad and pencil was continued until he tested his effort, now it was time to make the bag for tomorrow. After putting the next day's required books and note books in the bag he was to clear his writing desk and just when he had slipped the note pad in the drawer and pushed it back in, an image from the note book arrested his sight... What was it...? What did he saw ... Was it really that he just saw or what... a pause and then discovery of a quite new phase of life occurred, slowly he pulled out the drawer and there on the top page of the note pad an image of slanting wall suggesting of a stairs with details of bricks and railing he was shocked, it was exactly from the angle he had viewed one morning. Holding this note pad was giving a sensational realization of having this done, responsibility of an act, a string was co-relating this work to him and a new facet of his being. While turning some more leafs made him acknowledge more of the turn his mind had taken and more of himself. There on the other pages he found a design similar to the braids girls usually make for tying long hair in another image the sun was shown rising from the slanted stair wall. Now it was his turn to think. He has heard his grandfather discussing about conscious, sub conscious and unconscious he did not take long approaching his sub conscious mind gameplay. Just little did he know of mind's classification sitting right there stunned, how far could he think of that was beyond his experience, beyond vocabulary and beyond his study. The first thought after the fog of sensation was lifted came in his mind, was of his family. He looked at his father's portrait, he had long gaze at the portrait then with a sigh of relief he looked at the door as to see nobody saw that. He stood to gather an eraser to erase but instantly thought of why erasing it, erasing is time taking so he used stapler and stapled those pages while dong this he looked at his father's portrait with his head up. Yes he went to sleep triumphant.

It is difficult to segregate mind from our being, if our minds play tricks on us then two things may happen we shall be tricked or we shall catch the mind tricking us. It refers we are another and mind is something else. Perhaps it is a race between conscious and sub conscious; one occupies the other, and somewhere it is always the subconscious which reflects through conscious thinking...A very academic riddle indeed. He was tricked just when his mind popped the excuse "erasing takes time what if hide this in stapler pins". It did not take long when the pins started giving problem; they made writing almost difficult he had to open the pins while straightening each pin he was nodding to him as what harm they might bring to him. Yes love can never be harmful but how about a pre-mature love. A pre-mature love is something like pre-mature delivery. If love has nothing to do with maturity even this is an argumentative point but his was a snubbed one and unasked for one love for him, a love that was looked down upon with narrowed brows. There he was, filled with the remaining family to fulfill family dreams very straight way no space for love curves. It was clear with no disguised phenomenon that he caught him falling prey of love of the stairs girl he got it known, he proved smarter to identify actually to diagnose at the very out set and his preferences were clear so there shall be not a remotest chance for him to let him pursue silly emotions. Proved so tamed so much in self-control, conscious and careful Omer thus heading as being himself.

It is true that all the people do not surrender before love, for them love lies so below and they are superior, higher and fully conscious of their worth keeping utmost care of their self they actually fell deeper...in love. Same happened with our Omer. In some similar days a teacher had announced of a one day leave and their class requested to the senior head master that they do not require any substitute teacher as they had a test to prepare and they also promised that they won't be seen sauntering in the ground and will stay in the class quietly. It was unlike him but the headmaster had no substitute available for the period the one had been sent to another class and the second available one was already lending a helping hand into arranging question papers for the term tests a very confidential job so it could be easily allowed but the headmaster reluctantly said "Ok" very typical of him. There they were together had leisure to talk to share and to boost.

The top exaggerator Adnan added "You don't believe me! Ok, come at 6 pm spot us dating at the café" he also detailed the location of café and the seat location

"She comes to enjoy drinks from your pocket, see, she messages me" Sameer sneaked out his cell-phone, switched it on and scrolled for the messages. Cell-phones were not allowed in school but many would bring them secretly and secretly use them.

"Whom do you think spends…me? O no, babes spend on me that am, my style I am a killer"

He was about to stand when Nassir seconded him "he is right, now a days girls spend on dates my cousin got each time a latest model of cell phone from his girlfriends he never bought one"

Omer was watching them in harassment Ayaz was listening to them too, along with noting down some missing notes from another of his class fellow.

"What is the wrong with girls why they spend money where they bring money from" Sahir agitated he was short heighted and would give very childlike looks.

"Girls are cheap" Nassir declared.

"Girls are choosy they do not run after casuals but a killer they want, you don't understand" Adnan was about to expose something nuisance then instantly Ayaz turned the bridle and changed the route indulging Omer, Ayaz says,

"I guess special will be that girl who will capture our Omer she will be the gem of girls and Omer will marry her, so Omer! will you invite us all in your marriage see we all have elder sisters and brothers and we have no chance soon, we have time to wait but your sisters have been married and it is your turn now"

Ayaz summarized the whole novel and Omer bent his chin more lowly, class fellows did not enjoy this quiet reception of the comment and the birds of similar feather flocked together. Omer just reminded the best opportunity to finish comprehension homework right now and test preparation at home so he started doing homework at school's free period. Sameer went to Adnan's seat to seek advice of the love guru. Nasser remained sitting with another of his friend to curse the system in mutual tunes so time went by during which the headmaster gave a round and found the class in complete harmony and order.

This harmony could not prolong very long because the same day while their line was performing a turtle-walk show to the gates at the school off times the sun blazed in the shades of admin office waiting lounge and before he could look for detailed recollection she turned her face very abruptly infect in a noticeable manner. He noticed her noticing him and to make him notice that she was not noticing him at all, she started noticing other things (Did Akon sang *dangerous girl* for that situation hoo!). Was that real? The rest of the time until next day he stayed perplexed, same time came and he confirmed his doubt. Then many more days went observing her that she stands, fixing her eyes on him, then avoiding him, just when he approaches at the distance of six seven steps and about to exit from inner gates it was interesting. One afternoon he decided to observe the whole scene. He took a pair of dark glasses his sister's husband who was actually his first cousin, gifted him and he had not used them since, so he decided to make use of them, at the school bell rang for off times, announcement for junior to senior classes were made and his class turn came he wore glasses though his friends made comments on him but making the excuse of allergy he moved out from the class, now his eyes were safely fixed on the spot where under the shades of waiting lounge she used to stand. There she was, quite far from him but her eyes were fastened at him she was continuously looking at him without fear as it was safe to stare at a particular person in a crowd so there she was, constantly watching. The line was moving ahead very slow as the gatekeepers would allow exiting at a time one child to avoid any accident, so making each moment a million's worth she was watching leisurely he became bewildered, tried to look different ways thus he approached near and she bowed her face down. He continued the same glasses experiment the other day as well, yes the allergies do not go so soon. And today she had a teasing smile, it was appreciation for the glasses looks or he was looking funny but he noticed her blushing and with the nearing moment when she downed her chin he noticed there was shy smile. A feel of being worshipped he had for next few days. At this situation why don't the boys ask the girls "Don't you have father and brothers at home or can't you think of the honor of your father and brothers, why are you staring to a stranger setting aside all your modesty, is this the teaching you have got from your mothers" they can certainly ask because they know it is wrong their own sisters had been, and proclaimed very modest then why not the other, another girl should practice modesty. It is called double standards but the feel of being worshipped being noticed being waited upon or being cared for, gives such unmatched pleasure that a person becomes unconcerned to these concerns. Love is selfish! Some reciprocity changes do occur at his side. He became conscious of his hair set well, just at the school off time, he started walking more slow as to give and receive pleasure for longer limits, he made sure that the books in hand must be properly covered and for his face, the center of her focus, he maintained a fresh look with amiable expressions quick to crack into smile and laugh. Love takes to self-consciousness! Recently he adopted another charm which was to make her listen, his voice too, so just before the inner gates, when he was at the minimum distance from her he would say something to the boy ahead or the boy back or to the gate keeper of the inner gates loud enough to be audible even farer from her. She responded with more lowered face smile, still not looking at him.

Chapter 3

As for as loads of gifts are concerned they always had been heavy but today their weightage seems nothing in Mrs. Rehman's (Sara's mother) view. It was different today. Jimmy her nephew was on a visit, and it was all arranged to charm him, the sister along with her daughter were about to go back to UK when the husband of the sister and another son and his wife were already there., to make them keep remember, so the visit was most particularly planned, car was sent from office it was Rehman's personal car, branded gifts were loaded in the car tail special care was observed on personal appearance that was why Sara got to wear an outfit from boutique. It was 5pm and perfect time for evening tea when she reached her sister's accommodation

If casual becomes the antonym of care then it would be perfect. The host the sister of Sara's mother informed of her sister's arrival but out she was for window shopping, Jimmy was on usual hangout the maid was found after when these mother and daughter were allowed in through a male servant thus leading themselves to the back yard, as no one was there to welcome them through the drawing room entrance. Maid was busy doing laundry, their arrival though disturbed her but she proved kind enough to let them in by opening back side door of the TV lounge not only this but she also gave them the hope that she will serve tea when her sister the host will be back as per her orders. Sara's mother taking it a part of adventure more than the maid she herself was providing reasons of her sister's being out. It was for Sara because she could tell this to her father, for her own embarrassment or for being too cautious of the maid as they people report everything and she wanted all to remain, in the good books of her sister.

Another hour went Sara and the mother were bound to watch TV though Sara's mother tried to draw much information about different things from the maid as she would come to see them often in that while, in the meanwhile maid announced a happy news that Afia the daughter of host a little older to Sara has woken up and she is calling Sara in her room. Sara looked at her mother in response her mother almost thrust her shoulder saying "Go go your friend is calling"

Afia's room was paying homage to her favorite pop singers and movie stars, models with all accessories of sound system pc and the like. Looking all around the room Sara sat on a floor cushion near Afia and they both started watching songs. It was Afia's choice to replay any song so Sara was obliged to letting her sit with her in the room.

a two times she tried to bring study subject as a topic of their conversation but her cousin was interested only in talking about boys the news of separate branches of Sara's new school could not give her warmth though she asked in a very exited manner about her school, probably her expectations about a co-ed were higher.

The visit ended when just before some fifteen minutes to 7, her sister came back and the two had a sitting in which Sara's mother's main gossip was to appreciate each and everything of her sister's house including her insistence that the long waiting did not bother her at all for this her sister was on least remorse but all her questions about Jimmy were bounced with the un settled un easy life style of Pakistan. Later in the night when Sara's mother was sitting back in her home with her family her husband, her son and Sara she boosted how the two friends had long gossip and her sister was not letting her come back and insisting so much of having dinner together Sara exposed her ignorance on which her mother comfortably added that she was in Afia's room then and added that Afia loves Sara so much.

Whatever the unwelcoming stay had been there Sara found Afia's unbound details strangely; she updated Sara of her latest break-up. The reason was very complicated he the Afia's latest break-up guy could not sms her in response because he had recently got a position of internee and all he could do was a phone at lunch breaks. Afia could not bear this insult as to be considered so free to do one sided sms. She also announced to change her cell phone along with sim card obviously for new life and newer contact. But all this while she had to freshen up with new, and she had done shopping of so many music DVDs, Sara got her new feeds from here.

Whenever there is some family function and all the family members are invited that means there is something in the function for each member of the family. In some similar days Sara's family was invited to a family function. The biggest opportunity Sara's mother (Mrs. Rehman) could foresee was to see Jimmy and let Jimmy see them, particularly Sara, in her best appearance. Mr. Rehman Sara's father was more particular for seeking any session with elderly members of the family who in some such gatherings are always there and all together. Rehman was so attached to his late father and grandfather so an intimacy with elderly people was very natural in him. Zakullah, Sara's brother who was scolding her and snatched the sound system from her in the very early days of shifting he was called Zaki, Zaki *bhai usually, he too accompanied his family but to company only because he had practically no company there. There were boys his age sakes his cousins but he grew little solitarily, little more awakened because of a past tragedy their family had fallen to, and more care full more conscious and more closer to his father made him little more biased from the youth so he was him, with family and without much mingling. Sara did not come alone; she brought with her the image of the same second last of the row. She too did not want to mingle so much as the environment was rich with decor and beauty and she wanted only to imagine of him, imagine him undisturbed, each time whenever she would place his vision in the amid of that party suggesting some very good suit on him in the vision, she would always distracted by her mother, some cousin or aunt and she had to exchange greetings and promptly she would sit back to knit newer pattern of thinking of him. Adding more to her life for stock, for reserve for this moment and for many moments to come just that, because she was not sure or she had never thought of meeting him in real and saying things to him. She was looking pretty many aunts admired her particularly after knowing that their family has shifted to a posh area. He the second last of the row, was not there, to see her, to admire her, she was actually very lonely there. The function had to continue till late in the night. There was loud sound of music going on when Mrs. Rehman got to attend a call from her husband somewhat she understood and somewhat she made herself understand that her husband Rehman had to take one of the guest an elderly uncle to the hospital on sudden blood pressure shoot up and they, his own family Sara her mother and brother should request some relative passing nearest their residence to drop them home. This was a perfect opportunity for Sara's mother to make Jimmy drop them to home. It would be a dream drive when in the mid night moon he (without any family member, Jimmy shall be alone) and she also tracked all subjects of gossip with him of Sara's qualities she also had planned to give good hospitality whether he stays for a while. Tonight at the function she had hardly slipped her caressing hand on Jimmy's head during the social gathering where Jimmy too had to bow more low in front of an aunt to gain social popularity, so very excitedly, she was about to go and ask Jimmy to give them ride to home but her son Sara's elder brother Zaki stopped her from doing so, she was amazed to see her son was looking very angry he was looking just like his father whenever Rehman gets angry he becomes drastic. Instead of explaining why answers to her mother, Zaki was making phone call and in less than thirty minutes time they were heading home. The father of one of his friend came himself as it was not an appropriate time for his son to drive for another family. The next day brought a decisive day between Rehman and his son. The son did not do, not skipped any meal nor did he lock himself in his room he with logical genetics went straight to his genetically logical daddy and in forty minutes he had not only convinced his father but ready to buy a suitable car for him. Zakaullah spoke little about the rejection of the idea of having availed the ride from Jimmy that he should have or he shouldn't have at this moment perhaps there was nothing between two of the boys perhaps just the personality clash and nothing started.

Chapter 4

It was Friday and grandfather was taking start of his Friday preparations unusually early, he was to go to the courts, today was the hearing of his property case. Many things were unusual this morning, more than three times he went in the studies and it was not for the case documents but he would stand still looking at his deceased son's portrait yes Omer's father as if he were absorbed. A three times he caressed Omer's head before he was gone for school not only this but he also accompanied him to the school gate and he also prolonged his prayers there was a curious abruptness and trembling in his voice. After escorting Omer he made his way straight to the road to take bus for the court rout. If this is true that early bird catches the worm then his early preparation really worked and he got a seat in the first coming bus it was very early and many seats were unoccupied. Usually he the grandfather Siraj-ud-din gets seat, most of the times some good guy vacates to make the old man sit but at times nobody cares for the old man but that happened very rare. He was eager and now while looking out of the window vigilantly he was murmuring some prayers voicelessly and he stood up from the seat well before his stop and had approached the gate. The bus could cover half of his distance, so from there he had to take a motorcycle rickshaw to go to the road across the courts. Traveling and distance go along. Distances are covered through traveling then we may reach to the destination. Why they all sound alike, distance, destination, destiny, what is so common in them. If distance means time then destination comes for space then what destiny is? Travelling! Ok if time is consumed in traveling, reaching for a certain space umm destination so what is destiny then, travelling is hence an effort not destiny. Siraj-ud-din was making an effort an utmost. It was not for him, his own pension was much too enough for his meager expenditures but this was for his late son No for his grandchildren. Siraj-ud-din was making effort leaving all in the mercy of Allah perhaps destiny is the will of Allah.

It's been three years since Siraj-ud-din was pulling his trials in one then another and then another court, judges changed, case transferred to one court to another bus too changed its rout or gone on strike rain or sunshine Siraj-ud-din very patiently encountering case after case one for the succession then a couple of cases on his claim on the land he owns through succession and for self-ownership. The day his district got linked to the motorway the land prospects swore over a night. It became too difficult for an old man to hold his rights firmly when he has lost son, people knew he is alone and it is easy to threaten him and

grab whatever he had. Many times he had to prove that
he is the rightful owner, many a times he had to show up
his documents that they were genuine and once he had to
prove, that he is still alive. His younger son who was living
in Faisalabad doing business and besides much effort
he could not come to help his father on each hearing.
The younger son of Siraj-ud-din whose name is still not
mentioned did the biggest help to his family. He with the
support of his good natured wife and the obedient sons
got his both orphan nieces (sisters of Omer) married to his
both sons instantly after his elder brother passed away and
in this way he helped the family in the most secured way.
Omer's mother was very grateful for this help because it
would become too difficult to find suitable proposals for
her two daughters especially when their father had died,
leaving a house and no strong income generating source.
Their lands in the village could suffice to them a little
and settling down to this big city Lahore also lost their
contacts back in the village. The younger son of Siraj-ud-
din got little education and quite early he got married not
only this but Siraj-ud-din gave him his share from the
property of which he made the better use by starting a
business of cotton which his sons further promoted to a
brand and export business. On the contrary Siraj-ud-din's
elder son got education and did his LLB; he got married
later and died earlier. Sometimes Allah prepares some
people earlier as they are to carry the mission but carrying
a mission or sharing someone's burden is it their destiny
or dedication and all by the goodness of heart goodness
of heart is also a bounty of Allah.

Siraj-ud-din was more than usual worried because it was
to be the last hearing if anybody has to submit his claim

against his case so it was the last opportunity and Siraj-ud-din had natural fears though it seems unlikely but he was worried until his case title was announced. He with fear and hope entered the court room. There were hoards of people men women lawyers in black coats. His lawyer too was in black coat he very encouragingly through shoulders moved him little forward and made his space enough to make him visible before the judge. At this moment Siraj-ud-din could feel or sense nothing but all on his mind was the future of his grandson for whom he wanted more education and in whom he has invested all his dreams. He would recall the atmosphere of the court room the different faces with worrisome impressions the hold of his lawyer on his shoulder and every bit of the details of his travelling the weather of that day each thing many times while telling the story of this history making day but only if he gets it and there he got it. It is a queer state of mind when it is in trance like state, thinks nothing, but the one motif, later when the fog is lifted the same person can tell minute details as mother in delivery pain can later tell each detail of the day after she got her baby delivered is it the triumphant experience that sharpens the mind or what. He still did not remember clearly what the judge was saying to his lawyer but he was asked to tell his name then he was asked two more questions of the location of the area where his lands were located. The judge said something and the lawyer brought him out of the court room. the lawyer went in the court room again and when in next ten minutes he reappeared there was smile on his face he announced to Siraj-ud-din the happiest news of his life after the news of Omer's birth, the old man was trembling with joy and many mixed feelings, he suddenly gave up and broke kneeling down, trembling, his lawyer

who for last three year had been with him knelt down too
to hold him, some people too drew near asking the lawyer
what has happened to the old man, on listening that the
court has given the ex-party decision in favor of the old
man, many moved back as the old man they found him a
way ahead of them at least he had won, somewhere they
found them more in need of sympathy. An elderly woman
brought some juice for the old man which the lawyer
accepted with thanks and gave it to Siraj-ud-din. After
a short while he recovered somehow but he was so quiet,
it was the memory of the burial day of his late son or the
love for his grandson or perhaps the memory of his three
years long struggle days had wrapped him that for later
sometime he was quiet. Seeing his condition the lawyer
took him out of the court area hired a rickshaw instructed
the rickshaw driver and when the lawyer was about to
pay the fare to the rickshaw driver in advance suddenly
Siraj-ud-din recomposed and holding the lawyer's hands
he assured him that he is alright he would pay himself
then suddenly he thrust his hands in his pocket took some
500rupees and giving it to the lawyer said, it is for the
sweet-meat he also gave him dua for blessings the lawyer
accepted with a soft smile now he was fully satisfied that
Siraj-ud-din will reach home safely.

It was still early when he was back in home or perhaps
because he did not come by bus but by rickshaw so here he
was telling little and hurried again to the nearby market.
When he came back there were boxes of sweet meat he was
so excited to give some *gulab-jamun to Omer by his own
hand as soon as he comes from school, he kept standing
near the gate to receive Omer. Schools on Friday manage
with two hours earlier close as to perform Jumma. So

there he was, with Omer's return one could feel the breeze of happiness all around. Grandfather expressed his joy more openly to his grandson. Omer's mother, instantly cooked some meal, with meat and rice, she made the *biryani*. But before lunch the two of them the grandfather and grandson both went to mosque to offer *Jumma* prayer. Siraj-ud-din also distributed sweet in the mosque and exclusively to the *imam sahib* for his family. A phase of turmoil and test ended grandfather was more than relax, knowing nothing that a greater phase of struggle is yet to face.

The car purchase had been only a matter of yesterday when Zakaullah head straight to his father for his consent to send him Australia, he had all homework done already, his friend had sent him a visa to assist him in business and he had already got the student application filed for advanced business studies. Rehman was more than surprised he never had assessed his son would prove that faster to build his career. Though he gave permission, this time he did not take longer like he took on car purchase argument, yet Rehman was thinking that his son still needs to learn more of the world, more of the people and more about dealings but perhaps without this chance he could never learn that much. Rehman was stressed initially on giving a prompt permission, but only in few hours he was feeling very proud of his son that his son has the capability to chalk out his own map.

Omer was happy, though he was not completely aware of the fortune his grandfather earned by winning the case but because his grandfather was happy and his mother was happy and she was again and again thanking Allah

and telling Omer of His glory, the atmosphere of the
house suddenly changed, his uncle aunt, and his both
sisters, with their children came the same evening, to
greet them and to join in the happy moments everybody
was so happy that grandfather asked them to stay for
the weekend which his younger son (uncle to Omer) and
daughter in law agreed. The daughters hold the kitchen
and cooked delicious food and elderly members enjoyed
gossips. Omer's mother and grandfather's younger son's
wife were just like friends, telling many things of these
days and of past time also when Omer's father was alive,
this insertion although made everybody feels choked but
in the mean times Omer or Ayaz would come in, with
the children of Omer's elder sisters each time loaded with
chips, chocolates, balloons and each time insisting to take
them out once again, this visit was the most fun time to
them, the distance between Lahore and Faisalabad is little
but Omer's mother always encouraged her daughters to
live and serve whole heartedly in their in laws so it was
the first time that both the sisters came together with their
father and mother in law. The night preparation however
started late but just before Morning Prayer the doorbell
rang, everybody got up, for it was not long that they had
finished gossips and went to beds the extra bedding was
arranged in TV lounge. The women were more frightened
instructing, not to open the door and ask first, from the
inside. Just then grandfather's younger son keeping his
father and Omer (his nephew) aside approached to the
main door n asked loudly who is there. In response much
warmer louder voices came and he saying *ucha ucha* (ok
ok) opened the door and there appeared the two fine young
men, health and happiness was reflecting from them, after
embracing Omer's uncle who had come to open the door

they hold the grandfather and almost lifted him from the earth, while embracing Omer they both hold him for a while as to transfer lifelong trust and brotherhood the next they moved forward to the inner door this all happened at the gate way in the meanwhile the women understood who has come, women were surprised and extremely happy first the both new-comers bowed both their heads to receive motherly pat from Omer's mother then holding the head of Omer's aunt the mother in law of Omer's sisters in their arms they approached to Omer's sisters, and who could stop them after all they were their husbands but just when they were near their wives they took hold of their children from them who had also woken up and were now in their mothers arms half wake half asleep. So many questions and so many explanations were made before they properly settle down and another round of tea started. While at tea they revealed good news to the family that with their joint hard work and earning in export business they have finally enabled themselves for buying a double cabin four wheeler. This brought a new wave of happiness and they also explained why they were helpless in letting go their father and mother with their wives and children all alone in Daewoo bus service because they were engaged in finalizing the deal and until last minute they wanted so much to make the family move on their own big vehicle perfect for the big family, they two brothers tried much but the concerned person whom to hand over them was out of city and when they got it, they spared no time to join the family and to drive them back in own vehicle so excitement brought them just at mid night Their car could not meet their needs now, they also decided to hire a driver, to the four wheelers, and for their own use they still wanted to carry their car in use. Everybody was happy louder now as the younger blood brought boldness of expression after *fajer prayer all men came home and decided to enjoy a heavy breakfast so the two brothers took their younger cousin Omer into the double cabin to bring famous breakfast of *poori-chunny from some famous Lahore shop. Right after the breakfast the family from Faisalabad packed to move, the grandfather asked Omer's mother to bring those toys which they kept on purchasing for the children of Omer's sisters and they all went back happily but before leaving the home finally the family kept one another engaged in goodbyes talk in which women were seeking for the next visit plans and outside the house the two gentlemen were discussing features of their new vehicle with their grandfather who took a keen interest in knowing about the vehicle. While settling in the huge vehicle each took dua n blessings from the grandfather. They also greeted Omer and before another emotional session could start Ayaz appeared, the best friend, the neighbor boy whose mother yesterday came to see the guest and whom the children of Omer's sisters kept busy in buying trifles all the evening. The two gentlemen greeted and shook hands with the best friend of their cousin while they were asking of his studies the grandfather and Omer's mother had peculiar appreciation for the boy for his good bearing. The caravan left slow and they all, they all means grandfather, Omer and Omer's mother but adding Ayaz was balancing the flow of emotions so abrupt so they all witnessed them turn until the turn of the street end, grandfather was praying inside and Omer's mother was thanking Allah and feeling so grateful of his brother in law and his wife because from same this gate she had witnessed Omer's father coffin being taken to burial and soon after the departure of the two daughters married simply and now seeing them bloom was a new good episode, this all ran so swift in her eye that she forgot how much she prayed for the peace and prosperity for them, how much she thanked Allah and how much in past recollection, Omer forgot you! We have to prepare for the school quiz competition" Ayaz brought everybody back and the next whole day went casually Omer and Ayaz prepared from the flash cards and sometimes grandfather guided them.

Chapter 5

Omer was happy and before the weekend ends he became happier as the family visitation maximized the amount of happiness. Emotions need to be balanced and out flow of emotions make most sober people sometimes act foolish and it happens in case of happiness, perhaps humanity has learned more to confine sadness. It is a study of human behavior and let the experts make assumptions but one thing was sure in happiness one comes more to give, glee in greetings, and generous in granting. Recently he adopted another charm which was to make her listen, his voice too, so just before the inner gates, when he was at the minimum distance from her he would say something to the boy ahead or the boy back or to the gate keeper of the inner gates loud enough to be audible even farer from her. She responded with more lowered face smile, still not looking at him. But now he decided to give the precious thing one owns. It was right after the weekend of family festivity when Omer's team won the quiz competition and that day on leaving time, Ayaz who was also in the quiz team shook a warm hand with everybody in the class as to celebrate victory and thanking his class fellows for greetings when came to Omer, his team member while shaking hand a thought full sentence suddenly slipped without thought "See we are lucky together". This sentence induced more thoughts in Omer's mind and reflecting all events of small to big success he convincingly associated all, to her, knowing nothing of her advent seriously, and that day when his class name was announced he on the second last of the line waited it to move faster as he was to give the precious thing he owns. Suddenly he reminded himself of how, so the next moment he started talking louder to the boy at the back this could give him convenience to make sure that she has received it well over just near the inner gate the boy at the back shouted Omer *zinda-bad* (bravo) on this the gate keeper interrupted and Omer asked amusingly to the gate keeper to say the same for him as he has won the quiz competition today iterating his name, the gate keeper seeing this sober guy for years, happily chanted the same with blessings, then Omer turned back to make sure that it is heard and yes it was heard and responded with full smile in which pride on his victory was evolved first, but very next moment when she realized what she got today, the name! All of a sudden her world filled with his name and with the appreciation for the name and this all worked so quick that Omer could see her happy, proud, blushing and responding eyes with smile with all her being through, all her concentrated thoughts about him. It was difficult to say that who gave more happiness to the other. She received the name and he assured her happiness on listening, his name. A matter of reciprocation did I say love no, nothing in material was exchanged but the delight both experienced on that moment was so unique so pure perhaps the best metaphysical effects spring through metaphysical causes. That day after school both of them had little appetite, happiness was more there to fill, both got some work in their rooms Sara shut her in her room while Omer went to the study, that was his perfect snug, but life is not a snug at all for the very same evening when she was in the lawn, placing cushions in the lawn chairs whilst her father was watering the plants when all of a sudden someone belled the gate, her father had to go and see who was there. at first Sara couldn't understand the matter her father was getting harsh on someone bewildered she, better chose to get inside so while making hurry for the inside she also got her share of the scold "What are you doing here?" a scandalizing question spun her head, she was about to burst for explaining that she wasn't in the lawn for any rubbish reason. But keeping unresisting, as usual she flung inside. She knew she used to stand for someone daily but being accused for a thing she hasn't done was crushing her. And this all happened exactly on the day when he himself presented his name on the happy occasion, he won. Sara straightly went to her room and this time it took long to console herself. The fear of being caught while standing for the stare was muffled with the harsh image of a very suspicious father. Her train of thought went out-tracked and for the first time she was providing excuse to her aunt, her father's sister's act of committing suicide. All she had heard about her was from her mother that she ate poison in love of someone and her father couldn't forgive her ever. That was why she being a niece, bearing too much resemblance of her late aunt could not be left unchecked and unsuspected. They the father and the elder brother had proved more careful, than the care givers. That memory of that late sister sounded in all apprehensions and acerbic behavior. She was very much habitual of such 'also' citations, such references named or unnamed but at this moment her mind was the strongest advocate for the motive her aunt committed suicide. This life isn't worth living; why girls are born, and that her aunt should have eloped, because choosing an undemanding silent death instead of living a life with love could never earn her any pride to procure family status. She had been and will always be lashed so will she, being girl nearing to the age when her aunt did that and being too much look like hers. It took some more time to Sara to keep agitating until she happened to watch a video on some music channel it was song of Justin Bieber "as long as you love me". She watched in all possible times she could, it was latest one and the channel was running it repeatedly. That song worked for cathartic potion. For the next few days whenever she would come in her room she would sit at the side of her bed on the carpet laying all her hair bread on one of her shoulder. She wanted so much to write a note to herself saying "Meet me at the train station" but she chuckled at this idea. Now that evening scene was giving her perfect platform to visualize him that boy of second last of the line. No he is Omer, This time it was not the car mechanic boy standing outside the gate and being scolded by her father for not servicing the car but in imagination there was Omer, for the glow of sun set was giving newer charm to him because she had never seen him in the evening time and the villain image of her father, it was too, too perfect. One thing was also new she never took her father as villain or responsible for her aunt's sad demise. But while highlighting the hero ship of imagining Omer on the gate at sun-set, she had to accept her father a villain after all why he embarrassed her. Does love conquer all, means it devours all the relations, or is above all relations, or just being a loving one with good mood is enough and that boy Omer seems loving, she saw him amicable with children, many days past that way.

At Omer's house his mother was worried at his unusual long sleep because after school he had never slept so long. It was early November and days were shortening and it was in-appropriate to sleep until sunset, considered a bad omen. On sleeping unusually long, Omer was little embarrassed because this is the time which he used to spent with mother making tea for her with light gossip. The mirth he carried from school inner gate subsided a little. Ayaz had also come twice to offer him to revise for the test but he was sleeping. This thing made him feel more down. He was feeling more lazy sitting for another half hour on the same chair, would not make up to move when suddenly grandfather asked him to do ablution before leaving for mosque for *mughrib* prayer. On the way grandfather told many things which were new to him and he was surprised his grandfather was a friend of him. On way back he seems so fresh that he made tea for his mother and grandfather, he also fried some snacks. His mother was now looking relax his grandfather finished tea quietly as he was about to say something. At dinner he announced very good news in which there was a small assignment, to engage Omer in.

That night Omer had long dreams of open eyes of so many things the studies, family good, assignment his grandfather wanted to engage him, the girl to whom he was now associating with luck, with life, and with his own name. Then her face and expression, her smile at the confirmation on his name was unforgettable infect it was something to recall again and again for the whole of his life. He also wished so much to tell her how his grandfather won the case and how they all had been together last weekend, he also wanted to tell her about the children of her sisters, he also wanted to tell about his late father and he also wanted to tell that life had different facets and he also wanted to tell that she is a beautiful add among life's beautiful facets. Do we all want happiness in life and love pleases us? What if the same love pains us, is that still love, or what?

Love riddles are ridiculous, when she had been remained sad and agitated for some days seeking always to sit on the carpet beside the bed and assuming song acts, but this newer charm would not leave her sad any more, that was his name she recently got as a reward for her long patience long waiting of many long weeks. She wanted to recall every bit of that day. It was usual day after weekend same announcement for off timing for different classes and the last was made for the last class and there appeared him the second last of the row for whom she would stand, wait but when he would come nearest to her she would escape looking at him or consciously downs her chin. It was yesterday when she got to know his name not only this but she was also made known that it was just not the name but another assurance a mutual trust of non-verbal communication, it had begun. The excitement of being discovered was too high that she wanted to go abrupt with this newest pleasure, in the same recent she became more abrupt. The other evening when her brother came out after his packing to join the family at dinner and both mother and father were talking about his travel to Australia which was to take place next afternoon and gossips were going on about altogether changed climate there, she suddenly broke and it was not an appropriate sign when one is about to leave for a long journey and someone cries it is a bad omen so she was admonished and was asked to go in her room. This became more frequent the other day on not scoring an A+ on one of the class test, she cried so bitterly, putting her head down on the desk that her class fellows gathered round her, she never reacted like that before. Her crying made the teacher feel almost guilty of not scoring her right; however she spoke little on this except "*dil chota nhi krty*" (Do not loose heart, you are so sensitive). The following evening although her only brother had made his flight only few hours ago but she was murmuring some tune while arranging her tests in the file. Is this called hormonal change, Does it happen with every adolescent, Do they all react ridiculous? This ridiculous love's riddle could be solved if things would happen logically next to next but here it was November middle, winter season had set, send-ups plus house-exam were about to begin, and began the mystery of taking long walk at the girls branch roof early in the fog of the morning mystifying her this all new experience. More walk, more of thinking him was throwing her more inner of the love labyrinth. Her love or whatever that was experiencing had become an emotional suffocation. She had no one closer to share; no one could even infer the reason of her abrupt outbursts and to him she could never say those so many things in 'three words'. She needed a friend with open and somewhat liberal mind but one, in whom she could trust. She did not know her need but she sooner got an opportunity.

Opportunities do come sometimes we catch sometimes we miss. Later the miss proves better than the catch. He has let her listened his name or has given his own thing he owned personally but about her he knew nothing except she had the finest soul that she is shy, that she is coy, that she is intelligent, that she is innocent, that she is simple, that she is cute, that she has patience, that she has self-respect, that she has good taste, that she keeps things inside her, she keeps her things tidy that she is quiet, that her smile is cute, that she has long hair, that she has good middle stature height, that she remains silent, that she bows her head as if she consented that she wants to be owned. These days not in whiles but in wholes he would think of her. Omer has heard or not the lyrics of 'Hello' song by Lionel Richie but he '*has been alone with her inside in his mind*' (not the next line please) he could never think to mar her maiden beauty even in the dream; instead he wanted her to wait maiden until he comes for her hand. How, but Omer had this belief, that trust or that wish for her. An abruptness also appeared into Omer's day to day life. He became very active infect, hasty. Where he could go walking he would go running, always ready to bring grocery and in no time, climbing stairs to bring sun dried washings down, it was so fast that his mother had to warn. Not only in movements but his speech was also getting abrupt, while quicken away the time he would miss words from his daily speaking language. Half the line he would say here and half he would chant back while moving ahead. '*Kis bat ki juldi hy esko*' (what for he has become so hasty) a frequent line from everybody. If we could visualize him the instrument part of 'Hello' song could better describe his recently developed anxiety. He even started summarizing his answer notes in class tests, upon this; teachers took it getting casual to the studies. His class teacher took that seriously and managed a sitting with his grandfather and gave his figure out that the boy is after being in so much exam stress has become careless so he needs to become same actual Omer to retain his position, school prestige and family pride at this, Omer became alert but could not confine the other changes, they were supplementary growth, could not be curbed. Knowing so much about her, he still wanted to know because one day he got to know that he knows more about other girls of girls branch and out of school through the information guru of class Adnan and like him boys during fact revealing boys sittings, before assembly during break and any time.

'I have full profile record of every girl in girl's branch' Adnan boasted

'Are you a school office clerk? Impossible' Sameer's objection was full of doubt because Adnan happened to be an exaggerator.

Office clerks! All they keep is pass port size photographs, father's names and that's all I have access to all girls on Face Book. Adnan resisted

'From class 5th to matric there will be many thousands. Be real' Ayaz got seriously agitated.

'No, no, no. Not the kiddies I am talking about the senior the 9th the 10 the O levels and Selena Gomez and Kristen Stewart' this time Adnan was more in airs mimicking girlish.

'What Selena Gomez you have' intervened Sahir in a panic, only he could tell best reason why he jumped at her name.

'Look at him' Ayaz nodded his head in despair for Sahir's desperation for Selena

Before others could enjoy Sahir's situation somebody asked 'what are these Selena and Kristen do you mean for'

'You can't judge the fake or original what photos of themselves they upload on face book....' Adnan amused with shrunk lips and nodding head leaving the sentence, in middle.

By now all the boys have gathered round him with wide open eyes and slightly opened mouths as if they are not listening but seeing the information. It was not so that others were ignorant of face book usage each has conducted more than one face book profile such as for family, elderly cousins who always want their young siblings to be good smooth straight in the age when they themselves never were. So always a protective profile was for family fathers, uncles, cousins and the like folks. Then there was another for friends dudes date discussion sharers mostly of boys and a few girls of everybody's delight also used to be kept in the same account. Then a personal account comes which was to share personals with personal person. Everybody was listening keenly.

Adnan continued 'And I wrote on her wall that she was looking Cara Delavigne you know her massive eye brow I commented to make her sensible to pluck them a bit but she the nonsense thought I am admiring her' saying this he imitated sobbing by bending his head on a shoulder of the boy next and falsely wiping tears this gave boys a louder laugh.

'You are absolutely right, these girls don't have IQ' Sameer seconded in a complete sentence yet others were agreed the same.

'O listen, listen, listen' Adnan wanted to play more 'the other day the rest of my face book girls uploaded such weird pictures posing models you can't believe...' his half left sentence grew more enthusiasm in boys.

'And you know what, they take their own photos' Nassir added

'Obviously dude who else can capture these witches' another supported the statement, this gave another whole hearted laugh to the boys some were thinking of their make-over obsession, some were agitated with the in-appropriate out fits and some were laughing on their each time trying to give a new look through a new hair style.

The disclosures were on peak when in a challenge Adnan asked everybody to come his home and see personally through his face book account. More than anybody Omer wanted to go and see for him, he was devastated with the idea that all girls have clustered on his FB. That means she too is, no, never his heart sinks with the idea of seeing her on his FB. Anybody could tell the kind of girl whom Adnan had the access.

Chapter 6

That evening until evening Omer waited for Adnan's call, he also asked Ayaz to pay a quick visit to Adnan who was only three streets back but Ayaz took little interest as the gossip was a time pass matter and why must we take the statement seriously. It was a convincing idea but to Omer, it was his, like life and death no, but of his honor's matter. He couldn't wait so just before *isha* prayer he asked permission of his grandfather to let him go and fetch back his note book as it was for morning test preparation. In next few minutes he was standing at Adnan's gate where he was told that Adnan is not at home and at home nobody could tell when he will come back everybody was calm at his being out at this twilight. Taken aback, Adnan was observing a huge difference of life styles. He had to come back; worried, now more worried, he could do nothing. His mind was filled with horrible ideas, while making his way home he also imagined Adnan dating her, this vision was so crushing that his eyes filled with tear he clenched his fists and walking more briskly when he reached home, his grandfather was standing at the gate. The grandfather asked nothing except asked him to do ablution and escort him. They both went slowly to the mosque and towards the way home his grandfather showed him the patch of land. It was some three plots away from school and on smaller distance from their home but much closer than the mosque they just offered prayer. Omer had calmed down after doing ablution and further offering prayer and now he could think and speak perfectly normal. He liked the location very much it was like a dream come true, he wanted a mosque closer to his house for the sake of his aging grandfather. Both grandson and grandfather stood near the plot for some time his grandfather also expressed his wish the construction work sooner. While discussing his plans he told that the boundary wall at the far end of the plot will be demolished and there will be given another gate to the mosque so to facilitate people to approach mosque from the other side. This all was so pleasing. Certain other things were being discussed when they turned to way to home, suddenly a bike came flashing them from behind then after passing them a little ahead it stopped and then turned and came towards them and stopped. It was Adnan on bike after brief greetings he told that he was to drop his teacher's brother to the Daewoo terminal and his family told that Omer came to him.

'He went to fetch back his note book, he too have to prepare for the test' grandfather explained.

'Do I have one of yours?' Adnan's face was full of uncertainty.

'The STAT note book you asked in the last period' Omer managed somehow all that discussion was done in last period so the reference worked.

'O yes the last period' he slightly stroke his head with left hand, getting the clue.

'So the test you were talking' catching the string and tying up a knot, "See today in the academy teacher has given me the notes so why don't you come tomorrow after school at my place I will give you the photocopy and also guide you" almost conveyed the whole plan.

"But tomorrow he has the test" grandfather was concerned.

'No Dada G' Adnan pauses, 'can I call you Dada G? Seeing both grandfather and grandson, with an embarrassed smile, his style was so apologetic and so sweet that the grandfather promptly pats his shoulder saying affectionately, "Why not son, you are just like Omer"

Adnan smiled, half the work has been done he had won over the trust, "there will be no test tomorrow as the teacher says it will be after two days that is why he has given extra notes in academy".

"But how the academy teacher can postpone a school test"? Grandfather's amazement was logical.

"Because the teacher is same" both the boys spoke together, the first true statement.

Later, on the way home grandfather had made his mind to send Omer also to academy and get the extra classes properly as it is not very appropriate to go at some friend and share his notes for nothing.

The other day all day long Omer waited for the off time. Today when at the first school gate he looked at her, there was different look in his looks. He hardly could take lunch he was getting feverish, at Adnan's home he wanted vibrantly to make him see that face book stunt at first place. The time came Adnan went on proudly reporting each girl's portfolio, no it was not that the girls have exhibited, but the one which is perceived by the boys after filtering that into minimizing, maximizing, multiplying, analyzing and evaluating finally a calculated firm opinion.

'See this, she has changed her three IDs she also chats with Rehan and Nassir same flirt same lines, then see this she daily uploads a photo, earlier she was my girlfriend now she goes with my cousin, he has his own car that's why, here, here look at her she looks so simple and always sends me quotes I sometimes read them, poor she, she has got her engagement broken recently, leave her, look at this that is the item and you know what, when I accepted her friend's request all my other face book friends uploaded new pictures, yes, and you know her mother also has a face book profile, ok let's go to her friends list now, see, look that astonishing stylish mom, her mother has also uploaded her photos of her summer vacation trip to UK, I like her she is innocent but her mother does not like me once I went to her home, I do have bike only that's why.' Adnan could continue with his how story of hooking girls for hours together when Omer interrupted

'You were saying that all senior girls are in your face book record'

'Yes I said' Adnan looked in his eyes meaningfully, 'by the way whose profile do you want'

'I did not mean a particular one' Omer struck back,

'Ok, if you do not want to share it's up to you but I have presented all I have' Adnan wanted him to trust him and confide him so he did not insist to know.

'Have a look on all these again and make sure yourself' saying this he left the system all for Omer and left the room saying 'mother was calling I will just back'

Omer scrolled top to bottom than all the pages many times but could not find her, exactly that he wanted but now he wanted to make sure that she never was in his or in anybody else's face book contents. What his eyes were confirming it was alright but finally he was at the verge to ask straight yet he did not know how, already his class repute was of different built and he did not want to ruin that. He was in much ado. Omer had left the PC and sitting aside when Adnan came again.

'See dude all the girls cannot have face book or any such profile, sometimes their mothers are strict, sometimes there is no Wi-Fi connection, they have no mobile no PC or they cannot afford and rarely sometimes girls are genuinely pious, yes that happens too.' Looking deeply in his eyes Adnan further said, 'if you want some particular girl's information I can arrange, that's my promise' now it was Omer's turn to speak,

'No, I...I was just thinking you are genius you have got all the collection' Omer faked a laugh, 'But how you made this possible?' Omer invented another excuse to divert Adnan's attention.

'Simple!, here in school, girls are not allowed to talk to boys but in academy there is not much restriction and we have combined class, just accept one girl's friend request and other girls themselves send friend request, girls always are jealous of one another they are all the time in competition.' Adnan simplified a complex formula but Omer was not in the mood to enjoy.

When Omer was about to leave Adnan hold his hand, pressing a little 'you told nothing today but any time dude I can be helpful'

That was the moment Omer wanted so much to tell but saying 'alright then' he left, leaving his friend Adnan thinking seriously about Omer's crossword love puzzle.

The other day when Sara reached home her that aunt the sister to her mother whom they visited two months ago was now sitting in her home, her mother's delight was touching no bounds. The lunch with more food street items had been furnished on the dining table, the maid, the mother, the driver everybody even everything seems to born just to serve mother's that sister. During the lunch mother announced Sara with the excitement of a servant who is bestowed upon an order to whose fulfillment is an honor.

'Sara, go and check your room is alright Afia is coming.'

Next she addressed her sister saying, "It would be great delight if Afia stays here, it was a matter of two months only I still insist change the plan"

"What plans"? Sara was bewildered with the idea of having Afia in her room and that at the verge of her exam; Afia was a girl who will never let her study, study was some out zone matter for her she was interested only in boys.

"Afia has taken admission in a computer course that is of two months" looked at her sister for confirmation, "It is exactly in that academy where your school girls are going for coaching classes, all you will do is to go with the driver, pick her from the academy and come here" mother simply explained her duty.

"Then give her some company for two three hours, she feels very alone in home" her aunt first time spoke to her.

To Sara, "Then your aunt will come in the evening to pick her" to her sister, "let her stay, see Sara is so happy, both are friends" her mother's way was imploring toward her sister.

"I have to complete shopping and tailor visits so I have to go out daily… I will pick her… no problem" the response was perfectly plane.

Sensing her sister's, authoritative nature, Sara's mother turned to Sara, "Go and see your room is ok and at 4 you will go with driver to pick Afia"

It had been a week since Sara had to go to pick Afia, just when she wanted so much to sit and revise school studies. In similar afternoon, in her room Sara was combating with her thoughts about life and her rights, why was she born and if she is alive then why her rights aren't given to her as to other girls and daughters. That was her first confrontation since she grew a little and restrictions grew a more. Why right is not always right. If one thing is right for one person then why not right for the other as the same? This newer controversy ignited very first time two months ago when she visited her same aunt and spent some time with Afia in her room, weighing hell of the difference between the life style of her cousin with her life pattern. Yes it was a pattern and she has to follow but Afia, she could give styles liberally. Afia used to be encouraged on wrong things while she used to be curbed on right things. in Afia's room latest models of sound system, PC, LED, split AC and even a room refrigerator and to run all these appliance un disturbed, there was UPS too, and what best she would do with this lavish life style was to phone all night to her boyfriends on the contrary if she is up until late night for preparing a class test, her mother would come spying her, her father would get restless and her brother would straight away come and switch off the light, thus she used to be snubbed on an energy saver light usage on studies. Economically their status was similar perhaps her father had been more successful business man than of Afia's but she had too much limitations. This all new aggression ensued since Sara has to go again to pick Afia from the academy and then had to give her company and in this way daily, her three to four hours were being wasted right on the verge of December tests. She recalled the day when right after shifting in this area and getting admission to this school she once requested her mother to let her take the coaching classes to the same academy as the new school set up is faster and more demanding and almost all her class fellows were going there and she also needs to go to cope with, she was discouraged and the idea of going with the driver and the word of second time classes was carried so obnoxiously that she had to remain silent for the sake of her this much school routine might not be snatched from her. Her academy going wish was purely for studies sake she had not seen Omer yet. But now her mother is sending her there same for her own niece, she burned with this difference of attitude.

There was one more reason that was ample to think scornfully, that girl her cousin Afia whose pick duty was assigned to her and company giving job was also the part to that assignment, ruining her own test preparation, that she the Afia was not taking computer classes for any right reason, instead the boy who got an internee's job had the office next to the academy and Afia would go to date him in his lunch hour. Sometimes Sara had to wait for her in the car in the parking of the academy building and that Afia used to be seen coming back from a three hour date with some noticeable signs but with least remorse. This would crush Sara because whatever she was doing waiting, standing, and watching was so solemn and not without dignity. She felt estrangement even harassment in the company of Afia and the ideas of sharing secret, her Omer, never occurred in Sara's mind.

Chapter 7

The spade work had begun, early in the winter morning Rehman (father of Sara) noticed that the wall was being demolished and the plot behind the wall was being prepared for some building. It was queer that the wall touching their street had been leveled and whosoever is going to build must be going to become their neighbor. Rehman had recently shifted here for better and sound recognition and it was important to him that his neighbors must be of good class, curious him, one morning asked for the contractor to some laborer, After getting information, it was first time since he had shifted here, when Rehman felt a genuine wish to see someone in person, straight went him to the guided way and there he was standing at the door. The door was opened on first bell immediately, a nice young boy little taller than his own height was, wearing some school uniform, hair neatly combed and there was innocence in his face, age

66

something sixteen not more, "Yes?" his voice effect was clear, Rehman stood quiet, calculating the host person's decency with that represented piece, suddenly he reminded of the question he was asked in "yes" note and he instantly told the name of the person he wished to see. There he was welcomed with respect and made seated in the drawing room. That boy switched on the gas heater and went inside the home saying that he will just call the person whom he has asked for. After the boy had gone Rehman took an aerial view of the room. It was neatly arranged with old fashioned furniture. The sofa backs and sofa arms were covered with handmade Croatia lace (a lace made with special thread and one needle often used in making net laces). The center table was also of old fashioned make with Victorian legs. There was a book case at the left side with the collection of eminent poets, and scholars. Among them he could see *Bukhari* and *Muslim*, some volumes of Iqbal and also a *dewan-i-Ghalib.* The books seem to be the part of the family since long. There was a carpet and with a typical maroon rug in the middle. Nearest to Rehman there on a side table some old fashioned frames with black and white portraits and land scape of people could be seen too. A horse rider, two men with brotherly resemblance standing either side of a father like man. Rehman noticed that the same man was seen in horse riding then in a black gown either that was his graduate photo or he was a lawyer. In a brief view the family seems educated for last many generations and had seen good days also but now there was some still calmness though not poor but having no taste for show off, just maintained but not upgraded. Rehman was continued with scenic assessment when Siraj-ud-din entered through the drawing room door opened inside the house. That man in first looks looked impressive tall with slight bent on the shoulder yet his eyes were bright and his face bore seriousness of life's hard days, but when he spoke there was same clarity in his voice, Rehman stood to shake hands and about to give his account of coming here so early when Siraj-ud-Din asked him to sit comfortably and feel at home. While Siraj-ud-Din was listening Redman's appreciation and gratitude with humble gestures, the same boy entered with Tea and accessories in a tray. He laid the table very expertly and started pouring tea for both of them. Rehman took notice of the boy who was now wearing his school blazer. And the school badge was broached on his blazer pocket. Seeing him, noticing the boy Siraj-ud-Din introduced, "He is my grandson Omer he studies in the school, (he named the school). Omer promptly spoke and said Slam. This innocent obedience brought an appreciating smile on Rehman's face, "Which class?"

"O levels" he handed the cup of tea with much care. Rehman asked, while receiving the cup he asked,

"How is the school?" reserving the fact that his daughter also studies there.

"Yes it is good" prompt reply but brief, so Siraj-ud-din supported his grandson,

"School is very good he studied there right from the beginning, his two elder sisters have also did matric from the same, now they are married to my grandsons the sons of my younger son settled in Faisalabad", in old age the mention of successful and settled grand sons or daughters makes no difference but pleasure becomes equal.

"Dada g, may I leave now" Omer asked, "for how long your family is living in the area?" Rehman asked

Siraj-ud-din sensed that, while answering this question he had to mention his died son the father to Omer and early in the morning he did not want his grandson go with heavy heart so first he answered Omer, "Yes sure you are getting late, go from the other door seeing your mother"

"His father, my elder son, I bought this house for him, he did LLB here, than he got married sometimes in late 80s" earlier we lived in village" he averted the theme of his diseased son.

"So where is your lawyer son I wish to see him too" Rehman got excited it was another disclosure beneath this simple living. The statement of Siraj-ud-din could call two dimensions of the next question, he the Rehman, could ask about his living in village and further the land ownership, these town mover usually hold in villages, and the other question could be made on the person, his son, so by maintaining a question about his son he turned out to be a man who like to talk about person than property and possession. Siraj-ud-din did look down then up then smiled and not looking straight spoke,

"My that son has gone to Allah, now I am with my grandson all my dreams are for him, this mosque idea, (he continued) was my grandson's he used to say "Dada g you go far for the prayer I will make a mosque for you," slight laugh, "He is such a good boy", all this while Siraj-ud-din's first finger was intensely rubbing the sofa arm.

Taken aback with this sad discovery Rehman felt helpless as the old man was sitting with poise stating a sad affair and he allowed no consoling words through metallic tone, sensing his words will be too little or too late he joined Siraj-ud-din's left over string by managing, "it's great I mean if our young generation is so caring, it's great, it is all good bearing, my son is in Australia he has gone for studies and he is doing a business with his friend", assuming the linking the two examples is not that similar so he added, "today children have own choices, instantly sensed it was a negative remark so he turned, "how are you managing to construct it is a big project" Rehman finally found the track.

"Yes I had land back in the village after my son's death I also got the succession right of my son's share of property so it took three years to win the case and meanwhile the land value raised many times due to a government project was announced so here my grandson wanted to build the mosque first' Siraj-ud-din simply summarized the three tedious years of trial.

"I am very impressed, I also belong to a village, then my father started business, he involved me in, and we have also settled for some thirty years in Lahore, earlier we lived in another area then family wanted a big house so we moved here", it was a tip of the tongue reason which by perpetual usage he also started believing but living in the area with the cluster of family far and near persons have easy access sometimes may cause pain when the people keep on reminding one, how infamously his only sister died.

When we say something different and think something else the truth reflects from our gesture, he did not rub his first finger with the sofa arm instead he picked the photo frame from the side table it was like a gallant ridding on the horse,

"He is Saad, my son, he was the lawyer, and he loved riding whenever we would go to village he would ride a lot"

The voice of Siraj-ud-din was seemingly coming from some far, very dim instead another thing happened while Rehman was looking at the photo his image dissolved and another image grew clear it was the face of his only sister and in the picture she was looking very pretty in her Eid dress, that dress and bangles and all the accessories he himself bought for her and that photograph was also taken by him on an Eid event she was smiling, how come, was that an optic illusion how is this world of explainable physics such metaphysical un explainable things also do happen or is it the famous parallel world that exists a trillionth mm from us. Difficult to say anything, there was quietness when he noticed he was holding a photo of somebody's son whom he was meeting first time and he could not know that the old man Siraj-ud-din have stopped talking for a while and he was just looking down, each heart has its own throb so is its own pain..

The meeting summed up with another hour sitting in which Rehman very persuasively made Siraj-ud-din agree that the carpets, fans. Coolers water tank and toilet accessories will be his responsibility, already Siraj-ud-din is not availing any benefit of his contacts, in cement and other supplies arrangements because he had settled those all matter all by himself in much expensive rates having not used any contact, and most painstaking task to get permission from LDA Lahore Development Authority and other concern offices for the mosque built.

Yes obviously the two of them had become well acquainted ones and subsequently Rehman kept paying visits almost every off and on, not that early but whenever he would come, the both would sit for hours together sometimes until noon prayer and both would go together to the mosque. Rehman had special respect for elderly people, he was much attached to his father and he believed that in the sitting of elderly people man learns wisdom of the centuries. Here Siraj-u-din liked his love for the religion and good moral values he reminded him of the village life's originality, and there is not much surprise if Omer could go to Sara's house O I mean if Siraj-ud-din is invited to Rehman's house.

Chapter 8

When spade work begins, many an odd stones rough enough to be cast away are also discovered with the good for construction stones which are to keep. It was January end when finally Omer agreed to take some STAT classes from the academy teacher as per insistence of grandfather. He was almost confidant with his preparation but the grandfather was worried since the day he went to borrow notes from Adnan which was actually a lame excuse but grandfather seriously wanted him to cover if some work is left. Now it was decided that for some fifteen days the teacher will come Omer's home late hours like 8 pm after getting free from the academy, and Ayaz and Omer both will attend his class at Omer's place, grandfather arranged it so, he knew Ayaz parents cannot afford for extra classes. It was when Omer wanted to talk to his teacher for STAT for home tuition, Omer had to visit academy to take the acceptance of the teacher He was on Adnan's bike while Adnan was wearing a helmet, just near the academy he accelerated bike and stopped it by keeping some distance, Omer was already surprised at this un necessary panic but he did not know the panic was necessary because Adnan's cousin was coming out of a net café plus juice corner with…a girl. The both were so casual and talking so intimately, so personally, involved that they could not notice of being noticed the girl shook hand warmly imitating to hand-over a file with a file over her hand, and boy prolonged that hold, with his eyes into hers but they had to leave apart because the girl had to move forward to get in the car parked for half an hour on waiting for her with a driver and also with a girl, a cousin yes Sara. Both these boys Omer and Adnan, kept pursuing her with the eyes and now it was shock time for Omer because he recognized the car and also the same way sitting back seat away from the driver's back the executive seat yes.

Forgetting all about consultancy with the teacher, he posed such urgency that Adnan had to make a follow of the car that very instant. The car drove the two girls home and was parked inside, they both had to make short stop little away from that bungalow it was time when Adnan told the whole bitchy story of the flirt girl who was seen with his cousin and whose scandals were wide spread, Adnan was getting angry on his cousin at the same then he promptly asked why he asked to chase is he also involved?, here Omer left with no excuse and had to tell that it was for the other girl, "I have feeling for her" his first affirmation in a very serious manner. Adnan wanted to give a laughing break but seeing his serious face he simply announced

"I knew from the day when you came my home I understood that you are looking for someone and that you could not search, yes dude that girl is nice but her father is strict, he drops her school and that same driver picks her from school, she is innocent and she has no face book account this I can confirm for you."

"I know that is her driver but I have not seen her father, does she come with her father?" Omer was right, living in a home just across the school road, he never needed any hurry for school and Sara's father would take breakfast after dropping her to school then after reading newspaper sometimes after 9 or 10 he would go for his business, business community has late starts and sits until late. Once Omer planned to seek how she goes home he went to school again taking lunch for two, the two gate keeper as his mother, sometimes when, some good cooking is made, asks him to share lunch with school gate keepers so here it was the day to make mother happy and best chance to see her going home a little more than the daily episode but here she had gone with the driver only he could mark the car.

"Bro don't you worry I can bring her information for you" Adnan was proud of his girl tracking expertise.

"No you wouldn't do any such thing to spoil her name" Omer's response was an exaggerated one for Adnan

Believing nothing in, love, yet practicing flirts, Adnan insisted, tapping his left palm on the back of his head, "I know she is different and I have not heard anything about her but I can manage for your sake very secretly no one will get to know" forwarded the same left hand extended palm upwards as if to make a promise.

"You will not do anything like this I tell you" Omer warned, rather harshly ignoring his forwarded palm, Adnan spoke teasingly something worst Omer could never listen for her.

"Why are you getting so possessive about her just screw her and get the way out of it"

Burned Omer, crashed a burning slap on Adnan's face which burned him outside in Adnan did not slap in return, instead making himself settled back on the bike he simply said, "I can understand you are in love a clean and pure love and that girl is also innocent but see, whom is she with, if you cannot be of my kind than she should also not be with that bitch" he started the bike for his response but Omer was silent with bent head, Adnan raced the bike then he drove it back and forth to encourage Omer to sit but he did not move an inch...Adnan drove out of street and gone.

Some of the moments go very slow Adnan made his way to home within the same time-set but later that night he did not enjoy any cyber activity. Same time-set let the people go home, same time-set hurled birds to settle back in the nest and within same time-set the sun descended but that time-set lost its usual friction over Omer, not physically but mentally he grew many levels. Omar's heart got arrested in fears in worries in agitation once in the same while his animalism boiled him so much that he could not help thinking the same weird what tip Adnan just emitted, but thinking this same tip made him felt ashamed of himself, pulling himself through his this guilt, he dragged towards the mosque which had one opening in the same street, the same his grandfather was building. It was under finishing process, the workers had gone only a man from contractor was there to guard the material for night; however it was *mughrib* time so Omer did ablution from the bore water bored for construction. The water was unusually cool but Omer's sensory perception could feel nothing except this that he totally understood that he was helpless totally, in keeping his love intact from any wrong interaction. Sensing his being helpless he entered and bent he, before his Creator and while praying, while asking for the protection of the girl from evil of the society he, prayed so humbly, so deeply, expressing his nothingness, admitting his being powerless, acknowledging his love, chanting for the forgiveness if his love was wrong, exceeding in the wish to bring the same girl in his life perfectly under the religious order, beseeching for the pure safe stay of the girl until he could enable himself to marry her. And there he achieved the precious most point of concentration only which can give a disturbed soul, an immense peace. It was the point of retrospection how many tears rolled down, he could not see but how much spiritual lightness he felt after praying so hard, this however also could not be calculated but he felt filled, contended, protected. If the proverb 'Make hey while the sun shines' is relevant with time dimension then, that hey, also refer to the volume dimension, as much land as much hey but time spent in earnest pray certainly brings infinite volumes of blessings. Yes time is a real dimension but it can be set aside, many other of Omer's age might not be praying within same moment and the elevation that requires changing the destiny that is acquired through praying might not be granted to the others, all living in same time and space dimension...

Had he not bowed his head to the Ultimate Power that day he would have been swallowed by his own fears and impediments or the way he was getting reckless he had gone straight to her house in the frenzy of asking directly from her, the proof of her piety. These days the matric class was not coming, they were free for a fortnight only and according to the schedule they had to come to school for final test session in next week again for a fortnight. He spent this lot in praying too often for her though he had not been whimsical yet he misses her.

Some more days went by, the STAT teacher kept coming regularly, as per settled, Ayaz and Omer both would take the class at Omer's house, the finishing work of the mosque was on process, and grandfather along with Omer would go to see the mosque after the teacher had left. Adnan maintained his behavior casual, Omer too managed the same, only they would not talk together but in group nobody could guess of the row they had recently had. Sara had to pick Afia as the same and had to give time to her daily gossip. The only pleasure in her life was, of seeing him. Him means Omer, had almost lost because her class was given a week free before exam. According to the schedule they, the candidates of the matric had to appear for a final trial test session for five days morning and evening both to take the dummy test just according the board pattern, the school organized two tests a day of two different subjects and every single student of Matric or O-levels had to make appearance in both. The idea behind this was to prepare students of matric to take the toil and stay mentally stable to handle the stress for the second shift exam, and this was applied because they had been the day scholars right from their school beginning and they could mentally might be not ready for this change and that could be an awkward situation for them. So Sara was not there only for this week. Then she started coming, all matric was allowed again for just one week for trial test of two times a day for five days and then they were about to free finally. She would look tired and worried that was because exam were near and she was not getting full time support, yes she would look at him with the same steadiness but in all this week she had been holding some note book reading from it. It was so important for her to score a good result that the charm of seeing him had stifled in the fear of upcoming exam. Same was there after seeing her with that world famous flirt girl Omer would look at her, but only prayed, nothing went ahead exam toll was crashing.

The next week, one day Omer had hardly come from school and taken lunch when the door-bell rang, it was unusual because Ayaz does not come at this time and at the mid of the afternoon they had hardly any guest ever, luckily Omer himself went to see the door and there was him, Adnan with a very serious face and quickly blinking his eyes, Omer could least expect him, before he could ask reason of his coming Adnan spoke, "Today is valentine and every girl or boy must give gift or rose to their lovers if you want to confirm that about her you have to go to the academy road."

"To the Academy road …!" Omer followed his thought pattern without considering his own trust.

"Yes, Adnan spoke again, "the book shop, remember, just two shops away from the academy they have arranged valentine day accessories for sale you can check there now, I must leave my academy time has started," Adnan was genuinely in a hurry, so went he by

"Mother, the model test papers along with five year paper have now become available and my class fellow just came, he was saying that we must hurry for our sets or the stock will be out," he purposely did not mention the name of Adnan, "and mother he, my that friend was saying that the shopkeeper knows him so he has reserved a set for me, may I go to collect that mother?" Omer seldom behaves like that childish normally he acts serious.

"If he has reserved your copy then why so hurry, collect anytime" mother picked the right point.

Sensing his foolishness Omer began, "No mother we are fifteen class fellows in O levels and you know there are more other schools so if the stock will be out then we shall have to wait or have to go to Urdu bazar"

This worked sharply, sending the only son on a close distance was permissible and in next ten minutes Omer was there, Adnan too was there, outside the bookshop there was stall of old digests, fashion magazines, old enough to tell only old fashions and the like stuff Adnan asked him to sort the old books, while the girls will come out of the shop, the book shop was all decors in red with cards, heart-shaped balloons and teddy bear stuff toys, bear is such a wild beast if one chases that animal on national geography or animal planet. What is this wild beast has to do with love, who thinks, it has become a trade mark, that sells, inside the shop there were many teen-age lovers, and to learn the love-management many middle aged men and women also had gathered, teen-agers were buying and middle aged were seeking, for lashing the love, for aspiring a love, or just, for seeing the business of love was going on. Sara was in the shop, thinking this was so annoying and what if she comes out with a catch of gift or roses, Omer has confirmed the back seat of car particularly her seat was vacant. They came out, the girl whom was flirting with Adnan's cousin and the other Omer's life both came out the first who came out was Sara she was rather looking disgusted the way she flung out from the shop, she was not holding anything instead she had muffled both her hands in the mittens and rigorously muffled in a shawl that it was clear that her hands were busy enough not to hold anything, the next was that flirt girl holding packed gifts, a soft teddy and many more things the rose branch she had tugged in her teeth and she was looking more funny than to her expectation to give an image of some dancing-couple when girls clench the rose in the teeth just similar. Omer's heart under went three trials consecutively the first was literally about to result in a big bang (second version) its pounding exceeded when Omer was approaching the shop area then the second, it exceeded more when Adnan announced that he was just in time and the girls have just gone in and finally his heart was about to explode while he was sorting books, keeping his eyes on the shop exit, then came the another phase in which his heart resumed his natural throb once again seeing her empty-handed but it was a so brief that before the heart could feel rest after much exertion it almost flew without wings, to see the girl going clean, seeing his friend so much happy Adnan forwarded his hand saying "Won't you forgive your friend even today"

The prize for today should be really great but nonsense lovers never sense if that girl had no boyfriend that what is the credit that goes to Adnan instead shaking hands Omer embraced him, however this rather humiliated the both a two three scandalizing "voices" and of laughing they heard from around because in a day of valentine, two boys "so close" can deduce only one reason that both the boys could not have girl friends for them so they… Talking about heart, it is wonder that having experienced such a havoc shift in beating, lovers do not get the cardiac arrest. "Mighty is the heart that bears the love" it is not someone's' saying, Or is this nothing to do with heart, again there, and it is from above, no, not from the heaven above but from the top sphere the head, the brain exactly had it not been that Omer would never had accepted Adnan's friendship, again, so truly.

In another frame of friendship Afia, later that night after giving vent to her pent-up emotions on cell phone through a whole night package (strange she still reserved, even having consummated them in various hot-dates) O yes love is immense yes, and more is less here. So after 'that talk' she thought every bit of that day, her new dress, a Designer's outfit, her shopping for her boyfriend and then asking Sara to wait in the car while she went into another car parked on the next street and then in only 40 minutes she came back and while sitting back in the car she spoke loudly to make the driver hear "the system was held and my files were not saved so I had to rush back then there was electricity failure all my time went in that" at this Sara only stared her and spoke nothing. Afia also reminded of her in-different attitude in book shop while she was collecting valentine gifts. She could not think for long she had to sleep now because until 2 pm she has to get up for her so called computer class she decided not to take the class the next day so thinking this she slept with the plan of undisturbed sleep.

The other day Omer was extremely happy and that day he waited to see her more curiously until off timings because she has recently passed another test yet she was unknown to that, on that day Omer was planning to make her realize that she is good and she is different but he still did not know her name. same way like the day when he made her listen his name, so just the same he started sharing the curse of valentine day with the boy at the back, him was the second last as usual so again, just near the gate he made her listen "Good girls have no valentine friends".

This however, he could make with difficulty the boy on the back was in favor of celebrating valentine and on the passage towards the inner gate he had complete disagreement for he believed that we should not miss any chance of happiness, moreover celebration of valentine's day is not a perfect yard stick to measure the goodness of character. On here the patch of saying that good girls have no valentine friend was quick insertion in the discussion at this the boy at the back was surprised and this gave another chance to chant again the same line and then he also noticed there was smile, their eyes met from across and both were agreed on that, this all they both wanted, same agreements or disagreements. Love is what, all the self-love, do we love the one who loves the love we love. Psychologist disagree they are of the opinion that the healthy life should have difference of opinions so does it mean love is an unhealthy state of affair? Oops! Sorry. Let's continue.

Chapter 9

That was a different evening, Sara was unusually happy there was abundance of reasons; Afia had announced in a phone to her mother that she has discontinued her computer classes this gave Sara a sigh of relief as now she could study undisturbed, in Afia's company she would feel sickened. Once or twice she tried to tell her mother about Afia's secret of computer class but her mother snubbed her, not only this she asked her to keep listening everything, that Afia says but never stop her. Sara could not understand what her mother wants, if she also insists to keep listening her secrets and that without reaction, whatever, the other reason of her happiness was that Omer appreciated her that she has no valentine friend, only, she could not understand how does he know that, is he concerned, does he care this much? And he observes her so much. Well that was very astounding, once Afia told that the boys have ways to get perfect information

of girls, does he come to his street and keeps looking for
her, well this idea was much terrifying because it would
be dangerous for him too, as well. Does love mean caring
and worrying for the other the psychologist infer that a
person demands care in love, is usually been neglected
from affection of primary relations. Whatever, she liked
the idea that he tries to know her, and tries so keenly, what
if he takes rounds of his streets, no its dangerous but what
if he comes inside the house and her father, her angry
man father receives him, makes him sit in the drawing
room, and what if she cooks something and he gets to
eat that and what if ... there are so many what ifs and
sometime some what ifs just happen. The third reason
was a rare thing she saw her father very happy and excited
after a long time. He was home early and waiting for her, at
lunch, he was also anxious to tell her an exciting news that
he is contributing in the final procedure of the mosque
that was being constructed for last two and half months.
Her father also told that a pious person Siraj-ud-din has
started that work and now he is contributing into that by
supplying carpets, fans, coolers and accessories. He also
told that today he took Siraj-ud-din with him to select
design for carpets. "Siraj-ud-din is a very nice person,
simple life style, educated background and I wish to invite
him some day" his wife, mother of Sara was listening
quietly but Sara was listening with interest, her happiness
was that, her father was in good mood. Earlier his father
would discuss such things to her brother only, but today
when her father asked her to cook the sweet dish of carrots
she happily started doing all the work all alone. She took
little help from the maid and little instruction from her
mother but doing all the things by herself for her father
was so delighting that she spent all the evening in making

that sweet dish, kebabs along with pink tea best served in winters. Girls are always the daughters. It's true because the thing that filled happiness in her love was her father's an evening's good conversation.

That same day Ayaz reminded Omer of only two days were left in the five day twice daily morning, noon exam practice and O levels students were emphasized to take those tests for practice so like rest of the fifteen boys Omer and Ayaz got alert and the two of them requested their STAT teacher to allow them to do the self-study and They were right, their own finals were on May and it was just the assessment so teacher understood their problem, that day they had nothing to do with STAT so Ayaz went his home for test preparation. Omer also started studying seriously, he continued 4 to 5 hours at a stretch except for prayer breaks, then his grandfather came to him and very affectionately advised him that constant study might make him dull and might effect on his memory part, then suggesting this, he offered him for a walk. Walk with dada g had always been a love for him. In next five minutes both had been out. Grandfather had a good Kashmiri shawl so he wrapped that while Omer was wearing a leather jacket, his uncle, the father-in-law of both his sisters had gifted him last winter. He looked little more grown up and handsomer in that jacket. After visiting the mosque and seeing lights were fitted nicely with UPS (un-interrupted power supply) substitution availability both were very happy, to add more happiness grandfather also told the graciousness of Rehman who took him in his car right from his home and dropped him back too. Grandfather also told Omer that, they both went to select the carpet designs for the mosque. With Rehman, Omer had become well acquainted now, the one morning visitor, his grandfather often told him whenever that person visited his grandfather, and for Omer one thing was good in that person and that, his grandfather was happy in his company. After taking the mosque round up tour during which grandfather expressed his view about Rehman saying, "That man must have seen some hard days which has made him slightly hard but from inside he is down to earth, see he is buying all carpets and furnishing material all by himself but he insistently took me to select the carpets", saying this he started making his exit to the door opened to the other street, Omer interrupted, but grandfather had made his exit saying, "come lets go and thanks him"

Omer startled, "in this street?"

"Yes won't you say thanks to the person who had been all day long with your grandfather," grandfather's false pretense of anger, it was always so loving that Omer could do anything for that. They kept walking and the more they walked the more anxiety arouse in Omer's heart, "do you know the house?" Omer was filled with excitement.

"Yes, Rehman was telling, somewhere at the end" Grandfather replied reading every next gate's name plate.

Omer's heart, banging inside what if it turns out the same house, what if her father receives him and makes him sit in the drawing room, what if she cooks something for him, what if he could talk to her, and what if … there are so many what ifs and sometime some what ifs just happen.

For first five six minutes Omer took to settle his blown away nerves. Then trying to concentrate various things all together the first thought occurred, was that it was her home and she must come in that room to arrange and refine things, looking all over the drawing room which was defiantly equipped with modern lines furniture, false roof lights, expensive carpet and the like. Sensing that his eyes were doing a wander-lust, he suddenly fixed his eyes on the carpet, the presence of her father of whom he heard for a strict man, arrested him. Thinking only of what impression he is giving, well the first impression he had already given. Yet he was now scoring to his looks somewhat loosely. The jeans he was wearing was not a skin fit though but in good condition and of decent measurement, shoes were moccasins though old but well in order, the pride he was taking for, was his leather jacket, only last year his uncle brought for him, it was new and he would give a little mature look by looking little massive. Another word just sprung in his mind and he crossed the legs by resting one onto the other, that word was "body language" once in summer camp appearance speech his school principal made all senior section boys watch, a documentary on body language and postures and their effects on positioning the personality. Now Omer was looking very alert but all of a sudden another advice made him pull down his leg. Now both his legs were in parallel closer to one another and that was the advice his mother gave never sit in arrogance in front of your elders and here, there were two of them, finally what suit him best was to manage both his legs go straight, placing one shoe on the other, keeping both knees as much close as he could and fixing his shoulders with the back of the sofa but pulling his chin little ahead as to avoid arrogant look, he remembered how his grandfather would turn or lean forward his torso to listen the other and to give full respect to the person talking to him, with heritage now, he was in secure posture.

"How is your study going on young man?" suddenly Rehman addressed him,

"Good Sir, good", Omer wasn't prepared for this prompt plunge

Knowing well that the energy of his tone always shakes the confidence of the other, Rehman dragged him into discussion this time in a lighter tone, "I heard that they are running two exam sessions daily to train the students appearing in second shift"

Much for his relief, Omer was in his own ground, "Yes they are starting it for the first time and we O levels are also asked to appear, our exam are in May but they are pulling us too" his helplessness was so sweet that both the elders laughed.

It is so good so good for you, I must appreciate the school system they keep the students busy.

"Very busy, in our times there were no extra coaching, not much homework not so many test, Grandfather supported.

Rehman to the grandfather, "Yes but see today life has neck breaking competition" to Omer, "What are your plans after exam?"

"Plans..." before Omer could say, grandfather spoke, "they will go to village, there is school at our ancestral house I have donated that to an NGO, they will go to teach basic computer to the village children, Grandfather has kept such an exciting thing in his mind Omer was happy to listen that.

"They, You said who else is going?" Rehman was right in posing that question.

'His friend and our neighbor Ayaz, we will take the systems along with us and on coming back we shall leave them there to let the children practice over them," grandfather stated a big thing in a simple way.

"Great that is the spirit I am impressed", to Omer, "So young man, are you ready to take up this task?"

"Yes, yes sir, Omer smiled he was not trained to respond to such military questions in high moral pitch.

The aura of Rehman was so much occupying that for few minutes Omer completely forgot where he was, but one thing was for sure now he was feeling a lot comfortable.

The two favorite people of each other were talking on their favorite topics, with village literacy they picked the subject of technology and the shrinking world. Rehman was telling something about free Skype video calls on his cell phone and he was also telling how easy, has become the connectivity now a days when slightly a curtain rustled from the left back of them and a trolley was slowly being wheeled in. With that two persons entered, a man and other was for sure a girl, Omer dared not to look up he could see just the feet, and those could not be hers. It was revealed that both were husband and wife to each other and both had been living and working for the family for years. One more thing was revealed that all these servings were prepared by her; the trolley-table was embellished with steaming well garnished carrots hulwa spicy kebab, and home-baked biscuits, dry fruit and aromatic pink tea. Serving the refreshments the woman spoke very low to Rehman, "All these items, *choti-bebe* (the junior female boss means his daughter) herself has made, she did not even take my help"

"Sara made this all?" asking from the maid for assurance Rehman in a streak of pride and happiness spontaneously spoke his daughter's name then speaking to Siraj-ud-din he added, "My daughter, she is doing matric she is in the same school" glancing at Omer. Had he looked carefully he would have seen changed color and extra blush on Omer's face, at last her name was given to Omer by her most lawful owner the father.

I have no daughter, my younger son Muhiyudin also has two sons but Saad-ud-din had two daughters, his sisters, turning slightly to Omer, I think I told you, they also did their matriculation from the same school, after Saad's demise we got them married in early age to Muhiyudin's sons, now we have only Omer, well his mother is also my late sister's daughter,

"Late sister" some words only, sometimes crake icebergs of frozen emotions Rehman smiled, because he knew that Siraj-ud-din does not know, pressing Siraj-ud-din's shoulder he warmly announced, "You have your grandson, you will have a granddaughter-in law" both laughed whole heartedly Omer had nowhere to run he bent his head lower as if his focus was full on his plate, grandfather leaving his rosary on the trolley instantly hold a plate asking Omer, "You are eating all alone, give your dada g some". the maid helped grandfather in serving him, seeing grandfather enjoying the refreshments Omer took some more from every home made item sorry her-made item he holds big right over them after all Allah blessed him to have this. The conversation continued with pink tea for another 15 20 minutes then it was time to take leave of Rehman already 10 quite late for a winter night. The three came out, in the porch, the goodbye phrases were being exchanged when Siraj-ud-din announced that in the end April Omer's both sisters and children are coming to stay and the family is going to arrange a session of Druse-i-Quran and recitation of Holy Quran, exclusively for the women in their house and he on behalf of Omer's mother and sisters, invite the ladies of Rehman's family. Which Rehman at once accepted with great thanks adding "Why not, our families should also meet each other there are great rights of the neighbor recommended in the religion? Now the three had reached near the gate when just at once Siraj-ud-din reminded of his rosary, that he had forgotten in the drawing room. On this Rehman straight away asked Omer to go in the drawing room and get that as he did not want to discontinue when Siraj-ud-din was already about to leave.

When Allah bestows the volumes of his blessings they are in-numerable Omer could never have, even in his romantic most dream, imagined this evening, with no

special expectations he entered the drawing room again
and there, was she, standing just near the trolley holding
the same rosary, at this moment his distance from her
was from the drawing room entrance to the trolley table,
was exactly the same from the inner school gate and
the visitors lounge, and they had kept that distance for
months. Obviously and technically and logically and as a
rule Omer had to make advancement, so covered he those
few steps and there was she, frozen with the charisma
of that moment. It was not just him, to him she had
been watching, waiting, until then she had maintained a
moment's eye contact link but this was all new, different,
and never dreamt of never imagined of only a moment's
"what if" wish, which was the least possible probability,
but here was him. Do we recall on such moments, the
nearer to the nearest existence of Allah. Omer was
standing just in front of her and it was real while she
was holding the rosary looking at him un blinkingly a
statue, he hold the rosary from a far end of it saying "My
grandfather's rosary" here was only a natural distance
between the two people standing face to face while both
are holding one thing. Her fingers were only some beads
away from his fingers and there they both were on the
string of whose beads, for countless times, name of Allah
has been passed. The modern physics rejects somehow
the theory of particles of energy but it is the string theory
that has vibrant in the whole universe. The distance was
kept and the rosary was given and taken without any mess
only when he was about to turn to make his way back to
the drawing room exit door he finally made his full whole
attempt, "Sara ! Good name" leaving her bewildered when
he looked back while disappearing from the door she
was saying his name it was too low only he could hear

and it was for him only. The serving couple had sneaked out of the drawing room well before the guest departure for no good reason or just to avoid the laborious task of gathering the serving wares back to the kitchen, their laziness worked. Sara could continue standing same place, whole night in the commemoration of the moment when suddenly a voice shrilled, "Sara *baji* bring the trolley here I will wash the utensils, its already late in night" it was maid's voice she was sure that she will have an extra grab of food while closing down the kitchen function. Out near the gate the two could make another session of standing discussion, had Omer not had come out or had it not been so cold, the both could continue with their talk. "So Omer going to the village for computer literacy camp" patting his shoulder. Siraj-ud-din shaking hands with Rehman requested again to send family ladies at women Quran session, happily agreed Rehman saw them going, after giving a little escort to the mid of the street.

Chapter 10

A nother kind of shake hand was made when Adnan was sitting in the café, only smoking and alone, friends were taking the exam toll too seriously and that was stressing him more, he was prepared for the exam and he did not want any more of this so to avoid tension he came to the café alone. From nowhere one of his academy's senior boy made appearance and in next moment they were three of them sharing same table. The one from the academy was just a familiar face, that boy used to be overly dressed-up one in the academy. The other was a stranger to him, hollow cheeks, threaded forehead, neatly done eye brow curled lashes, skinny, stylish out fits to which he was carrying very casual. Throughout the meeting he spoke very little the familiar academy boy playing for a spokesperson or a middle man introduced him as an upcoming model, a very busy person and the reason why they both had to come around him was to avoid some agent of a female model who is hankering after him to agree him to sign a project with her. the excuse he spoke, was much professional and more scornful, that "She is over-aged and I do not want my career ruined, supporting her" all they both wanted was to agree Adnan to take them saying it is urgent and sit in their car, later they will drop there same. Getting bites of fashion world and further relating them with added spice could be a so much fun and Adnan boy was already getting bore with the echoing sound of exam, exam, and exam. They did not drop him just the "later" but late. They drove him to their place. It was a big hall on the upper floor of a beautiful big house in another posh area, more posh area. The model boy turned out to be a rich-man's son and that the familiar-face the academy boy was his friend, partner in business and more…..

"How did you start I mean how your father agreed for that" Adnan was shocked the set-up was so luxuriously furnished and because no father can allow his son to run a set up for the boys to play billiard on betting, betting on car-drifting, drug supplying. In an answer to such question, that stranger the model boy who was seemingly trying a pose on billiard table holding the cue, came slowly near Adnan tapping Adnan's shoulder, spoke ironically 'We must listen our parents keenly, it works" looking meaningfully in Adnan's eyes who was looking up to him as he is a new mentor for him, when could not understand, the same model boy angled his cue to the same familiar-face academy boy to relate him the whole story, (as if speaking in details tires him and he hires people for this job) perhaps interacting in detail mars the mystery of a model whatever, but the academy boy told the whole story taking start that his (model boy's) father's favorite actor was Robert De Niro, his father would insist him to watch his movies then once he happened to watch one, "Taxi Driver" the model boy inserted with his hand gesturing a sign of a loaded gun using his arm, and there he found the secret of keeping things in drawer bottom he continued, the next he went to his father's room and located same drawer hiding, "Dollars" the model boy spoke in a swing the worthiest part of the speech it was brief and effective he knew the ingredient of a perfect model. The middle man boy (from the academy) in supporting role spoke that there he got started his new life, new business and all that.

"And the fear of something I mean law" evidently Adnan was so much under the emphasizing hold of rich lavish life-style that he did not ask a straight why question instead he spoke the word of law very low it was the order of that place. "Success", that rules" again the model with a brand logo. Making the things simple the familiar academy boy simplified that boys come here to chill and if somebody wants to crash on billiard table or on car to car deal we do not mind, "neither we force" inserted the model's arrogant style by now he had seated on a comfy chair resting his feet onto a table-top "and the drug we have, is for some special guests" the middle-man boy continued, "Do you also offer hookah," asked Adnan timidly for Adnan hookah was a big thing, the academy boy laughed "hookah", it is a girly thing we have manly items here man serves man" he winked or it was Adnan's illusion. "Tell him we will deal in dolls soon" model boy changed the position of his feet on the table top.

After having this meeting for many days, Adnan could not stop thinking the idea of bringing his friends and common-girl-friends there. He could have the access over there, he was to enjoy, it was something like leading his friends to a richly place as an explorer himself what a boost getting the gossip of showbiz world from a person inline, could play billiard, could enjoy big LED, free smoking of expensive brands, full time electricity, luxurious set up, there could be no better hang out than this in the summer season, but he had exams, now he had an incentive for the exam end. But he continued phone contact with the same academy boy the middle-man and on each phone that boy told him the benefits of introducing new friends and attractions in stock for them.

The trial exam of morning-evening shift went smooth with no new happening. Omer had to appear in those, as per school authority decision to sharpen the exam vigilance skill more in the O-levelers. If nothing happened unusual, than the same nothing happened, usual either. Both, they could not see each other during this exam trial. Technically logically and as a rule something newer should have happened after the episode of visit at home, the new brings excitement. "Excitement is the spice of love or else love rots or recedes", Remember, it is not someone's saying. After the home visit experience psychologically both of them wanted more, what more?

The more also happened it was the last trial-exam day and also the end of the February, and also the rain, heavy rain continued all night, and during the last paper time particularly. The matric and O Levels both had taken their last paper of that day's second shift. When they came out it was so perfect for the growth of love themes. The rain had stopped; very cool air was blowing announcing yet another rain fall soon in the night. The green of the school area with the patch of red bricks all had washed in rain, combination of red bricks with lush green lawn and the misty grey sky overhead was replenishing with the ideas to the inspiration seekers. But the most exciting thing was that deep grassy ground which was not allowed to tread by any, in the school just near the inner gate and providing a festivity of the view to the visitors from the visiting lounge had now filled with rain water and had become a pool. There came out Omer from another room allotted for exam just to eliminate strangeness associated with exam hall environment. Walking his way to the inner gate no, not in line today, just got the sight of her, Sara's. far across the pool she was sitting on her knees doing something, beside that pool, this girl always dazzles him with all new surprises, one thing was sure that she was not sitting this way on her knees for nothing. Omer slower his pace and at a safe point giving himself a cover of a tree across the same pool stopped, he was curious, what is she up to, watching her doing something was itself a joy he had never experienced yet, so there he was and in next moment she carefully launched a paper boat in the pool water. It was so sweet and so innocent that he could not refrain himself making a show up from behind the tree, admiring Sara with an encouraging smile. The boat was fast flowing towards his side of the pool, all of a sudden he bent down too, now it was for Sara's surprise, when he could find nothing he made a paper boat out of his question paper that was given that day. He should have done something different, boys are less innovative, and who said this? No, nobody just continue. However his boat did not flow towards Sara the flow was towards him so it quivered a little then floating little ahead stayed with an extended root of the tree, now both Sara and Omer were watching their boat-show with much more comfort of corresponding looks. It was time when some other student or peon or some teacher on duty could have walked that way everybody had to go home before another rain and they two, also could not prolong their stay, already Sara had opened her pencil-box scattered all pointers, pens, ball-pens on the floor to imitate gathering them in such an awkward situation on the other side Omer did bigger he dipped his one boot in pool water, now he was pouring the water out from his boot-vessel, somebody might ask how his left boot went to swim in the pool when pool was on his right foot, nobody asked world is busy. The boot prank somewhat disturbed the water waves and gave Omer's boat terrible jerks but it did not sink, Sara's boat also made a curve a stop-short and then fast it flowed to the Omer's boat and in next moment both boats were safe next to each other amid the old tree roots. This childish game gave both a lot of pleasure and seeing both boats together finally, both went home very happy but what they could not observe that day and how they could, it was just a game but it reflected their lives, in coming days.

Chapter 11

It was the first day of Sara's matriculation exam. Her examination-center was a nearest government high school for girls. Her father had dropped her early in the morning, and he too had gone to his office, only Sara's mother was alone in the house. It was the usual case of routine life but after reciting Quran with the dua for Sara's good paper she went lost in the chain of recollections. It was because of her exam, it was because she was in Sara's room or it was because she had just done an intense prayer, all through the years since her sister-in-law (her husband's sister) died infamously she had been keeping a strict eye on her daughter more than the usual. It was not so that she had no trust in her own blood but because she had assessed very early, right with the death of Sara's paternal aunt the same suicide sister-in-law that the example she has set behind her, is so horrifying in the aftermath and it will be her daughter alone, who had to face the re-defined values and strategies, slings and arrows of watchful eyes and critical comments from all around. Sara's mother and her sister-in-law were good friends, her sister-in-law was the only female member in the house when Sara's mother came as bride in Rehman's house, Rehman's mother and father had died earlier, and her sis-in-law was a school student then. With the passage of time their friendship grew, Sara's mother got two babies subsequently Zakaullah and Sara, meanwhile the sis-in-law got her admission in the college, Sara's mother had to pay more attention to her infants sensing her sis-in-law studies are serious she would not force her for long sittings of gossip neither she had time spare as the new babies filled all her leisure instead she would ask her to study. Sara's mother could not notice that the isolated time she provides her sister-in-law was being consumed on another kind of studies and more than her, her sis-in-law tries to sneak in isolation. Later it disclosed she was doing some other study. It was her first year when Rehman was suggested of a very good ambitious son of another business man for his sister, he agreed, and asked his wife to ask his sister, sisters and daughters are appreciated to stay shy and modest so often such things are asked indirectly, the thing was still did not disclose as the sister did not clearly tell her affair with the boy in the neighbor and who was about to go abroad so she only said to Rehman's wife that she wants someone whose future is linked in living abroad, well it was not taken seriously and many examples were provided that business men go on tours more often so her this excuse did not work. It was the time she the sister was completely helpless, during all the time that party (the family of the boy from Rehman's business circle) kept on asking on phone about the choices of colors, the measurement of dress for the girl because they wanted an engagement in prompt. Rahman's wife would go on shopping daily, her brother (Rehman) would see the shopping admiring his wife's choice and admiring her good heart for her sis-in-law. The house had become a place fully functioning for a pre event time, concluding the sis-in-law was left with no say. On the same day when the engagement was about to take place she heard someone saying that the boy's family wants the engagement replaced with the nikkah a legally affirmed relation no back-out. Some of the elders of the family who had been invited a week before the event convinced Rehman that he should not think for delay, sisters or daughters always are to be gone so today or tomorrow that is no big difference. Agreeing Rehman had to arrange for the nikkah registrar officer, the witnesses with national identity cards, and more arrangements more food and many more things to be done for this lone brother-cum-father, how he could observe… Rahman's wife was busy in entertaining the staying, and arriving guests she also has much to do as the function turned into more big nature so to make the bride ready for the big ceremony was also her responsibility. She was trying all familiar beauty parlors to get the appointment for the bride-make-over on phone. Her two little kids Zakaullah and Sara were almost neglected. It was when she reminded herself to bring the dresses for the kids down from her room upstairs and to give them to the maid to dress them up for she was not sure when next time she would be free for them as the day ahead was to be hectic that was last time she saw her sister-in-law. She was going downstairs with washed hair dripping water through them, "See these hair will take time to dry, go get my drier from the room first," saying this she turned away and when she looked her next, there was foam from her mouth, her lips bluish, and her face has got pale with no breath, she was taken to the hospital on an instant but it was already LATE. Later Rehman mourn why he kept intact all belongings of his died parents in their room even their medicine; some attachments detach us from some other attachments. Who said this, don't ask it is serious .... It was some ten or fifteen days, since that suicide took place, when her husband, Rehman would continue sitting late on the roof and would not come down to sleep. And when he would come down he wouldn't sleep but kept on sitting on the chair next to the bed and whenever she would ask if she might bring him tea or milk or anything he would not allow her nor would he allow, switching on the light perhaps in darks of the night he used to shed tears. And very soon she understood these tears have found their exact theme. They were not of the loss of a sister a younger sister gone in early age but those were of revenge against that so called lover-boy, against whom he could do nothing the elders of the family comforted him realizing him that in such an action the defame of the family would go wide-spread instead the elders suggested to remember only that she got the stomach pain appendicitis, could not be relieved and went. Then those tears were of the disgust, how and why his only daughter-like sister broke his trust. He would keep on recollecting that he had been so helpful in making arrangements of her admission in college, in sending her for shopping and even to her friends' houses for visit particularly after their parents had died, he had become a father to her, but she did such a shameful thing and right over her engagement. He also sought a suitable husband from among his business circle, but she proved so

inconsiderate, it was so crashing, more he would think the
more his pain exceeded with the details of the loss he bore,
she did not think twice what her brother will have to face
in the society and what pattern she had left to follow, again
there so the whole toll of her loss befell upon Sara who did
not know the higher sensitivity of her aunt's action. Once,
after one year when Rehman was little able to talk about
this, "We cannot blame any person or society that is our
daughter to be checked", said he, he meant to say my own
sister but what was conveyed to Sara's mother that was so
alarming that she, and not anybody else, she adopted a
policy, a plan to cope. With growing Sara, She made Sara
a home-bound, no friends, no hang-outs never sleep-
overs, concentrating on studies, while perfecting her in
kitchen and other households she would herself do
shopping for her, yes she would always buy best wears,
best accessories of the dress but making her stay home not
only she actualized but also publicized. To more comfort
to her husband she never allowed her to get extra coaching,
she never encouraged her to sit long or even talk long with
father or even to her brother, knowing well the mind-
frame of the family males. Instead she would accompany
her in watching TV. That was the routine she scheduled
for Sara as long as she was to stay in her father's house. She
had even brilliant plan for her daughter's superb exit too.
She actually wanted her get married to Jimmy her nephew,
her sister's son because she could sense well that getting
her married in the in-laws will begin an endless lashing
on her, people in the in-laws still refer her so much
resemblance with that aunt in a suspicious way, so it would
be a hell to marry her there. Rehman was right in moving
away from the family, shifting here, because of their
frequent reminders through this way or that way. People

style of asking used to be so safe, "What was her age when she "went" was she of Sara's now age?" nice people in using a soft "went" instead saying loud yes she committed suicide in love of a boy, they pierce more. Estimating both girls ages would give another scandalizing meaning. Sometimes somebody would ask softly, "Does Rehman mention her sometimes?" as if he has forgotten so one must keep reminding him, another reminder, some would bring information of the boy or his family proving their faithfulness with Rehman's family but inside an effort to ignite the fire and enjoy a spectacular of another ruin. So it would be disastrous to get her only daughter sent to the soul slaughterers. The idea incorporating in marrying her Sara with jimmy was to send her away as far she could and they the jimmy family had settled in UK long before her own marriage, their first child was three years, when she married to Rehman. She had a dream that her daughter live a liberal happy life over there, she had seen her sister the mother of Jimmy had been very happy so, for years she had been paving the way for this match the gift episode, undue favor to Afia, time and again pouring, boast of love and care of her sister in the ears of Rehman was all strategic in effects. She proved so diplomatic that even in her mother, father and sibling family-circle she would always speak in favor of her that sister because she knew reporting agenda is very fast, moreover she had stopped visiting the family persons whom her sister did not like much. While arranging Sara's room shelf which was already well arranged she opened the frame in full it was a foldable frame and could show some and hide some pictures. She stretched it to the full open. There was the picture of the same sister-in-law on the last eid occasion, last eid of her life, she was beautiful and Sara now was giving perfect resemblance of her. Rehman's wife had never been biased with her sis-in-law; she still had her suicide note safe with her, she had always had sympathy in core of the heart with this girl, all she wanted her daughter's unblemished happy life.

Chapter 12

It was more than a surprise for Rehman that his wife's sister was here to propose his daughter for her son Jimmy; he always thought of her an arrogant, conscious of her rich life and that she had always under estimated her sister, his wife, so it was beyond his perception. He knew that she had got her elder son married to a UK national girl and she keeps low opinion even about her own relatives in Pakistan, she rarely comes, Pakistan, once in three or five years' time so it was much unexpected for him. He was right she would never propose his daughter nor would she ever had thought of that, it was all what Rehman's wife reported him after her typical editing work done. The actual thing was, she did not come to propose and nor did she propose Sara ever. Rehman's wife managed to invite her by ensnaring her in a deal being done privately for the few ladies of classy choice, it was some artistic designs of Indian jewelry and some pure silk saris brought from Bangalore and some similar items of genuine quality but in non-negotiable rates for exclusive ladies. The snare gripped fit, she came earlier than the expected time and the both visited that lady's house. The sensation was a bit true but most of the material turned out was local and a retiring model, seeing her career declining, has got them on sale. To provoke her sister Rehman's wife whispered she had bought some items for Sara, well she had not. Provoked sister got to buy three items each for her, her daughter Afia and her daughter-in-law the UK national. it is usually a custom to see and discuss the shopping after it is done, so came home they both, naturally to Rehman's wife home there they discussed that shopping and shared the memory of many more stoppings done from various markets, from UK, from the people personally acquainted and other success they both had made in their task of shopping. Sara's mother was giving wide edge wisely to her sister to boast big things with more support of heavy high tea; obviously everything was planned for this visit. While the discussion took a turn to the children she very warmly asked or suggested or posed or encouraged or implied no, not implied very straight away unstoppably, said, 'Why don't we get in a relation your Jimmy our Sara how would be that, I am sure we two families will be a great success together, set the rest of the family aside just we two you are settled in UK our Zaki is settled in Australia same life-style, same status, what do you say isn't that great", Sara's mother applied all logics to exploit her sister's weaknesses.

The answer was not in clear NO yet she (Rehman's wife) understood the way her sister straightened her back with the back of the sofa from a leaning forward posture, it wasn't enough her voice also lost hose and she suddenly looked at her wrist watch saying "But Sara is studying", before she could announce her meeting with the saloon for new dye of hair Sara's mother played her trump, "See Afia and Sara both so good friends Sara never told any secret of Afia she cares her a lot she never told even me, only once Afia got her purse slipped and it opened and things fell and I got to see some,(she brought close her mouth in her sister's ears and spoke the name of a thing that men use for protective measure)", I tried to ask but Sara is such a faithful friend of Afia she never told, only I got to see that" however this part of discovery was true, Afia's purse once fell opened and all the same just in front of Rehman's wife, Afia's mother was not listening the faithfulness of Sara but had been stunned at the unfaithfulness of the time, the situation, that impelled on her. smoothing her nerves and looking at her nails she also cleared her throat and took start, "Who else is ours such as you I mean to say Sara is studying but she will remain my daughter yes" she was trying to escape but Sara's mother tied the other string with this loose end adding, "Then we should get them engaged the sooner the better brother Asif is also here from America on a short trip we will invite him too, what a happy gathering and see we will not invite anybody from x colony (she named an area where, their, still poor relatives live) ok you give me the list I will invite on your accord what more? You will leave for UK after engagement and meanwhile we will do all preparations and then we will give great reception on marriage, ask Jimmy to invite all his friends on engagement and on marriage I will invite myself all his buddies (she purposely used the word buddies it was Jimmy's fond word for his friends. Jimmy's mother yes the sister of Sara's mother suddenly straighten her head from a bowing down position of deep reflection and said with a spark, "So, well we get them engaged", listening this, made Rehman's wife flung in airs, "First you take some sweet meat, and to Sara's father I will myself tell this news that my sister is asking for Sara, when shall we do the engagement?" logically this question should have asked by Jimmy's mother. "Sara's paper had they finished? Jimmy's mother asked estimating some time factors still thinking to escape, "Yes some practical tests are left, and they will be over within this month, (that was April)" she was trying to give maximum edge to her sister. "But we need preparation, after all some of the things should have prepared", Jimmy's mother applied the same weak point of her sister's recent promise of festivity of the event. "so please you decide preparation are also to be done and time is limited" ignoring time factor, "How about end of May?" she knew she had return flight with Afia and Jimmy in early June. When the sister of Rehman's wife was leaving, Rehman had come, they both exchanged casual greetings while Rehman's wife was excited to make her sister say same things of engagement to her husband but she kept reserved rather hurried in leaving the home, so Rehman's something more than surprise was right.

Just before the May, before the exam of Omer, his sisters, their husbands, the cousins to Omer, the children, both uncle and aunt to Omer who were the father and mother in-law to Omer's sisters and primarily the younger son and his wife to Siraj-ud-din, arrived for the weekend. They came in the same double cabin big vehicle along with the casual car. The whole family was busy in the arrangements of that women session of Quran recitation and *durse*. This year they had more to spend so more arrangements were done. Previously a thorough cleaning and washing of the house, sometimes white-wash of the walls and flower-pot painting used to be done to celebrate the occasion but this year the family had bigger plans. The carpet of the drawing room was to be changed and new curtains were also to be bought and in all this, one thing was decided that women will go and select the design, then men will go to pay and collect so the first group of women, in which Omer's mother, Omer's aunt (the mother-in-law to his sisters) and both her sisters were included, was taken to the market of heavy items of home décor and furnishing along with jewelry, dresses and marriage accessories. It was after many years, Omer's mother had the trip of that market, and the market had developed in much more facilitation. Omer's mother did not forget to take the mother of Ayaz with her as she always had accompanied her to shopping of nearby markets and this time she also wanted to compare rates of different items with her estimated amount for the dowry of her first daughter who was soon to get married in some months. The ladies selected three styles of carpet with same texture just with the difference of color and similarly some curtains were seen and finally selected for the drawing room. They got the samples to show the family males to collect those same. After this Omer's mother bought some decent bed-sets for the grandfather, and some more to display on occasions and she planned to spread them on the day of the event when many guest ladies from the neighbor were about to come. All the ladies bought crockery individually for their homes, of exclusive designs to serve the guests. The shopping ware was being sent safely by the shop porters to their double cabin. Now it was time to buy new dresses for the daughters and their mother-in-law (the wife of Omer's uncle), that lady had been so sweet and loving to them how could Omer's mother forget her biggest virtue in taking both orphan daughters as their daughter-in-laws without dowry. Omer's mother always wanted to give some good gift to her and it was the occasion when recently after the final settlement of the land suit in their favor they were in much financial relief so as a token of their gratitude she had made up her mind to buy something for her to which the grandfather happily agreed and gave Omer's mother a good enough amount. They had to cross the road all five ladies together, the shops of dresses were across the road so here they (the three senior ladies) were, strongly holding the hands of younger women (Omer's sisters) intending to protect them instead being protected by the young blood. Each time when there came a little chance of crossing the road they would pull their hands towards back signaling it is still not the perfect time to cross the road. Most feared was Omer's mother, both the younger women were also in a state of panic losing their being-young confidence with each vehicle gone by and them waiting for the 'clean and clear road'. One or the other of Omer's sister tried to convince, "When altogether we will start moving there will be the way," while she was saying this a women with her maid appeared, maid carrying bags for her, they crossed the road in a swish. The reluctant group was watching them in amazement when suddenly their sight caught a young girl, too young, like a school-girl, who was also with the lady and maid group, just stood, still, amid the road. The Omer's family's group was in a what to do situation. The girl was looking lost or in some mesmerism, fixed, not trying to escape; perhaps she had taken the speed of the road over her nerves and was struck. That was not the time to discuss her numbed nerves. It was the time to help her, she had been having hair-breath escapes and it was too dangerous to reach for her help. All of a sudden the most feared of the group, Omer's mother moved forward, leaving rest of her group behind, and holding the girl through the shoulder, just dragged her, she made the road crossed with her, the bewildered group of daughters, their, mother-in-law and the neighboring woman (Ayaz'ss mother) quickly crossed the road and joined them. They the daughters were about to say something to that young girl for whose safety their feared mother just plunged in but Omer's mother calmed everybody down saying, "She is just a child must have frightened, see they drive so speedily, then to the girl, Are you ok, Where is your mother? Shall we take you to her?" the girl had managed to get little control, assured them she is alright and her mother is just there, pointing to the ladies the same two, one, and the other carrying bags the maid, were now on the stairs of the plaza. Seeing the girl gone and looked back with a slight wave and thanking smile for the mother of Omer, they also made a move to the next stairs leading to the dresses. The girl and those two ladies went through the stairs towards the jewelry shops. The women group soon forgot that all, but one of the sisters of Omer phoned to her husband who drove them to the market, she asked him to bring the vehicle nearest to the plaza.

Chapter 13

Had she and her boat drowned that day in actual, it would have been the best end of her life, because if in this life she cannot be his, than she cannot let anybody's else to be hers. Day and night thinking the same Sara now had, had hallucinations of Omer. Now he is coming, and now standing in front of her. Sometimes imaging all her incidents when she could see him so easily when they could look in each other's eyes, or when he made her hear his name, when he came her home in real just when she was just thinking of what if and that happened in actual, thinking this much made her cry, more sad, why such a miracle does not happen again, why it was so brief in her life to see him and why not only her face but her fate too resembles with her diseased aunt. For last few days when the phone had become busy, the news of her would be engagement had set fire in all the relatives, Maternal and paternal both, when the shopping work had begun. Once in the evening she heard her father expressing his fear if they (the Jimmy family demanded for the nikkah at the engagement occasion), this lost her thoroughly that night she stood under the shower and stood for hours at a stretch until the water tank emptied and she got the higher fever, it could be a sign for the parents but instead her mother took it only an effect of some evil eye and gave alms and charity to remove the evil effects. As for Rehman's satisfaction Rehman's wife made him talk to her sister on which she comforted him that such a big occasion could not be held without her husband's presence so he should not worry. But inside somewhere Rehman was worried the matter was being settled and solemnized between ladies he was expecting at least a phone call from Jimmy's father, each time his wife calmed him inventing different excuses. Once he became successful in making a direct conversation with the father of Jimmy in UK, he was very happy at the engagement announcement and he assured him of his happiness lies in his wife's consent, and that she had been a good match-maker the elder son's wife the UK national girl was also her selection so he, like a typical easy-going, happy-man-version a contended husband expressed his joy amiably. He could not be blamed for any responsibility in future related to this engagement. Sara's situation was getting worse, early in the morning her mother announced that she had to accompany her to buy jewelry, the ring, for the ring ceremony, the gift-able jewelry and the like. Sara was most reluctant; she wanted to take her life before wearing a ring of somebody else's name. Sara's mother took the maid along and the three went to the market for the marriage accessories. Sara's mother was extremely happy her dream about her daughter was about to come true so in the fervent of joy she was a bit faster in pace while her daughter Sara was more than reluctant. On crossing the road when her mother and her maid had crossed the road she being slow or her mother being over-excited ignored that she was left a little behind, she just stuck in the middle of the busy road incapacitated of listening, thinking, or reacting just numbed. It was an intentional step for suicide or she had lost any more strength to drag her soul less body. She had been seeing things happening against her will and she knew she holds no power over them so such an intense incapacitation sometimes would throw her in the fog of hallucinations and sometimes in slight mental paralysis, (a state of inability to react), the minor examples were like sometimes she would think to stand, or to sit or to walk just to get water or to reply but she would not, the willingness that sends the message to the body to do, to perform or to act physically was losing its hold. This stage if continues, takes the patients to slow death when their appetite (the strongest motivation of willingness for life) is lost and then they do not need expired medicine to take their lives. On the road on just middle of the road she was standing with blank looks insensitive to the voice of traffic and crashing speed of the road. She could see all around and her mind was telling that this is the scene of the road but her mind was numb at alarming her that this is not the right place to stand still, rather it is killing, this could continue unless the whole story would end with her life right there but, there hold her someone, from the shoulder and pulling her forward, almost dragging her escorted her safely to the other end of the road, gasping, she still with blank looks was not fully comprehending this moment's energetic ebb that flowed actually in her favor. Some girls were saying something but the same

benevolent lady, caressing her head with her hand said,"
"She is just a child must have frightened, see they drive so
speedily, then to her, Are you ok, Where is your mother?
Shall we take you to her?" this gush of voice and physically
been drawn somewhat enabled her to sense the severity
of the situation, she assured her that she is ok, while she
moved she wanted so much to tell that lady, the unknown
lady all about her, why, perhaps she had retrieved all her
conscious so instead she just looked back, waved with
smile. Omer was also a brief happy patch in her life, so
brief, in jewelry shop her mind numbed again.

Both groups of women reached home late, male members
were in panic. The children of Omer's sisters proved
much naughty than the usual opinion about them, the
reason there were only males left behind; the father
(one of the father, the other went to drive the vehicle
for ladies), one grandfather and one great grandfather
and on the top their only maternal uncle the Omer, so
children took much liberties from these apparently male
but insidly mild creatures. The children were used to of
their mother's frequent beatings throughout the day, here
in the absence of that motherly order; these young masters
were manipulating the fatherly law by exploiting their
loving care. Until they had come back the kids had gone to
Lahore Zoo, to Mc Donald's, and then to the Play Land of
Siddique Trade Canter they bought many toys, and many
a times the senior fathers had to blow air in their balloons.
The greatest job the male did that they put them to sleep
before their mothers had arrived. To the other group of
women on shopping when reached home, Rehman refused
to see any shopping all he wanted to make sure first, that
the ladies of the house both his wife and his daughter are

going to attend a session of ladies in Siraj-ud-din's house the day after next day. Rehman had promised already now there had been two three reminders from Siraj-ud-din; Rehman's wife could not afford to offend her husband moreover she was also curious to see the family of whose simple and sincere manners had impressed Rehman so much.

It was a good suggestion and was received happily that women of the house must not be bothered to cook instead the food will be made available from the catering service providers and that with each guest food shall also be given as take-home-packs. This was decided to give ladies of the house free-of-work hours to join the Quran recitation and *durse* along with the guest ladies. The house was giving a brightly new look from inside, there was new carpet, new curtains and new bed-sheets in all bed-rooms with some new serving crockery. This year's celebration was bigger as the family had recently got some financial ownership and the best they sought to thanks Allah was by sharing more food and happiness with the people. The session was to start after lunch and Ayaz sisters had already come to help out in the arrangements and there was no wonder after all they had been good friends of Omer's sisters and had been together in the school, only they the Omer's sisters had to get married earlier. Men-folk were outside the house in making the arrangement of food and its perfect distribution; children (children of Omer's sisters) got one more day to rule the men.

"Where are you going, come here, when shall you go to collect the cold-drinks" called Omer's uncle to one of his son,

"I gave the order yesterday and that man was saying he will himself come for the delivery", his son said

"No, leave that, they always forget you go and collect yourself", "alright father," "also bring disposable glasses", his father Omer's uncle gave another reminder.

Now he spoke to his other son, "what are you doing, where are the *Nan* (the thick bread)", the other already sensed his father does not want the men keep standing on the passage from where the ladies had to pass, so he immediately handed his younger daughter to Omer saying to Omer, "her mother was calling her, she wants to change her dress" to his father, "Going, almost gone"

"Gone where? First unlock the car Omer will keep the children in", his father assuming it the perfect to keep the children in one place, saying, "Yes, see it is unlocked, to Omer "If they tease you set them right", however he knew Omer would never beat them, instead Omer used to suggest his sisters not to beat the children so often, and he left too.

If somebody has ever thought that the children may be 'kept' somewhere, in peace then it is wrong for only in fifteen minutes they got bore of listening radio, and watching LCD of seat-backs, well Omer became successful in putting two of them to sleep and not to make the noise of wakeful ones awake the sleeping twos, he sought best to take the two wake-full out, now the two were sitting on the bonnet and both were trying to exercise their power (this word 'power' they heard from some cartoon character), by pulling Omer's hair and by punching at his chin, to which

Omer was keenly receiving. It was the last occasion for sure when Sara could see Omer again and for the last, this time again he was all busy in childish pranks looking same innocent even more than the first sight, she happened to see him. The two elders grandfather and Omer's uncle had almost turned their chairs already from the entering door, Omer's head, hair, nose, chin all were occupied by his nephews when Sara came out from the car, in this much while when her mother Mrs. Rehman was instructing the driver to come again in next two hours Sara got some things confirmed, first the him, he was standing beside the bonnet and was busy with children, second that those children were his nephews and that, that big vehicle was of their family's she heard standing there, "Its Omer *mamu*'s car" children chanting, "No its your Papa's car" Omer correcting, this drill continued three four times when Omer surrendered, "Ok ok its Omer *mamu*'s" now go in and get changed and come back I am waiting" Omer applied this trick to make them agree to change their dresses, "Then will you take us to shop?" a condition was put forth from the children's side, perhaps negotiation is an inbuilt phenomenon of human beings. "Yes, but only if you get changed" Omer exploited their shop craze. So went they in, meanwhile Siraj-ud-din stood up as he recognized the driver was of Rehman's so he received the bouquet and fruit basket from the driver, politely guiding the two ladies the drawing room entrance, he entered through the common door to place the flowers and the fruit in the kitchen.

Chapter 14

The session continued for hardly two hours. After the recitation the prayer break of *Aser* was observed than the durse started, it also continued for an hour and then the final thing the *dua* was held and all the ladies did *dua* for the solutions of life problems collectively. Just with the end of *dua* the food was served, Ayaz sisters were ahead of Omer's sisters in serving the guest ladies, while ladies had formed a natural circle, in which new members were introduced and the sugar and blood pressure status of old members was asked Sara's mother sensed it, an impolite thing to keep her young daughter sitting with her whereas elder girls of the neighbors were on serve, so Sara also stood, went in the kitchen and kept serving trays of fruit, rice, curry *nan* to the ladies. Omer's sisters had recognized her, for the same girl struck in the middle of the road but they did not remind her of that instead they kept asking small questions of her school interests and routine through that, they were fully convinced that this young girl had little exposure so getting struck on the road was a probable matter. Sara also saw children of Omer's family and she twitched their cheeks to avail a once in a life opportunity with her dream family. She was not numbed, she was not lost instead she was receiving this all with whole heart as for the bounty of Allah that in the series of days when she was about to get engaged, she got this opportunity to see him, to visit his home, and to talk to his family and also leaving good impression as for his sweet memory. Earlier when she was coming to this house she was happy, very happy and she wanted to stay happy all that while and she did not want to spoil this moment by thinking of her unwanted engagement, so she got ready earlier than her mother and wore a nice pink dress. She was looking more pretty with the extra glow of happiness, but here after the session was over in which Quran recitation, prayer then *durse* then *dua* was done her soul got an altogether new dimension, during the *dua* session she also did *dua* for her, and for Omer, for both the parents, Omer's parents, and for her own parents, and for their life being together under the safe canopy of the parents. She came here happily and she went back with hope. When there, no reason is left for hope, only then the real hope works and that is the faith in Allah Somebody has said it or not yet the believers believe that. The children, taking her for an easy aunt just like Omer uncle, insisted her to draw and make some things out of the paper. Paper, they just made Omer to buy for them. She quickly drew some images of children's interest, than to each child made a toy out of paper, a cat, a tree, a flower a car and they were running all fours to show up their toys announcing, "You know Sara aunt made them" as if everybody knew Sara, to children we must not tell a lie and when children asked her name she told, but now everybody got to know even Omer got to know that she has left Omer far behind in pleasing the children, and had become children's favorite, now the children were all on her side. Omer's heart was won again. A man wins a women's heart just once, and a woman keeps on winning man's heart all through the life. Nobody said that? Strange!

The grandfather was just coming back from both the mosques after distributing the food there, leaving the supervision of distribution of food management task on his son and grandsons, when from a distance; he saw a young girl was standing near that big vehicle with the kids around her, aside from a cluster of women, who were gathered round to say goodbyes. Assuming it is the time of ladies leaving for home he stood by the wall in order to give them a safe passage. Standing right there he noticed that same girl in a hurry, joined the group of ladies, and when each family was leaving she also left in a car with her mother, and that was none other but turned out to be Rehman's daughter, and her name was…was yes her name was being resound by the kids inside out 'Sara aunt Sara aunt', she made so many things with origami art to please the children. Children escorted her to the main gate with more demands of toys and promises of her soon return. Before the grandfather would go in he wanted to make sure all the women had left, so he went to the chair that was drawn out since evening for the house gents, a little aside from the entrance though present at the service if needed, before he would sit again all of a sudden his eyes caught a sight, what was that, curious he went near, near that big vehicle, where a few moments before Rehman's daughter, children's favorite Sara was standing, and there, under the wipers of windscreen, was tugged a boat, a paper-boat. Siraj-ud-din carefully pulled it out. He was looking at it appreciating, thinking such boats they would make in their childhood now a day these things are taught in early classes in the name of art, carrying that boat he went in, to give it to some child.

Early next morning the family from Faisalabad got ready to go, hardly they stayed for the breakfast with the request if grandfather allow them to leave their small car with grandfather as that will be convenient for Omer and Ayaz to reach their examination hall. Grandfather highly appreciated this offer and accepted with making a demand that right after the exam he had plans to take the boys to their ancestral village with some computer systems so he will be in need of the big vehicle then, to move to the village. "Worry not, that will be there at your gate with driver" His son promptly replied, the idea of village computer literacy filled enthusiasm in him., the family left in the big vehicle assuring them to send the driver back as soon as they would reach. Left they, leaving bundles of good memories, like always Omer's mother praying for their safe travel and always safe arrival. Grandfather too stood, praying watching them gone and then came in.

The O levels exam time went well, the driver, Omer's cousins had sent, was staying in their house and it was so easy for both the boys to attend each paper at an examination hall located quite far from their area, the last paper too went well and on the same day the driver went back to Faisalabad to come very next day with the big vehicle for village adventure. Everybody was very happy and relax. While the boys were taking the papers, grandfather would take the elder brother of Ayaz to the *Hafeez Center* for the deal of computers for the initial learners, that brother of Ayaz had real technical and professional knowledge about computers, he was an admin officer in some IT department of some private company, so he suggested for the best deal. Everything was going well. The focal person from the NGO was also very happy on this personal involvement of the donor in the literacy project. It was the same NGO to which Siraj-ud-din had donated his parental house. Now a days summer vacation is going on and there are no students in the school therefore no teaching staff, is available but he promised that he would call each child right from his house to join the IT workshop with the help of his social mobilizers, this he told on phone to Siraj-ud-din.

Chapter 15

Some knockings, if answered lead to diversion, disaster, dread and damage. Omer answered the knock and opened the door and there was him Adnan, "Just come with me" why always his way had been so mysterious and occupying that Omer could not resist, Omer knew that only he knew his secret so anything for her. Worrisome signs on Adnan's face made Omer half faint already. After reaching at the end of the street Adnan explode, "She is getting engaged'" Omer wanted to think he is saying about someone un important and not about her at least this news, but his sixth sense made him more panic, "Who?, whom you are talking about?", Omer demanded with fear in his eyes. "She, your girl, you have feelings for," Adnan reported in the same wording as Omer once told him about her. Omer's life's, worst shock after his father's death, because after this news if he would have to live, there will be no life. "And you know to whom she is getting engaged, it is the brother of the same bitch who had been flirting with my cousin, my cousin told," the reference was solid, "It's today, my cousin had just dropped her to her home from the beauty parlor in his car" another shock for Omer he could only say "Today" more he could not say or listen or even feel because he collapsed like a sack, Adnan had to make him sit, but he was losing. "You want to cry" Adnan said to him he had hid his face in his sleeve his body was in jerks anybody could tell he was sobbing. Seeing his friend's this worse condition Adnan got disappointed, the spicy information he brought about the family of the boy for his friend could not be shared or enjoyed. Adnan was getting worried then helping him stand he said to his friend, "Come, come, just come with me" Adnan was struggling him up and when Omer removed his arm from his eyes, they were red as if they wept blood, Stunned Adnan, holding both his arms he struggled him to stand then taking him through shoulder took him to his motor bike asked him to ride, Which Omer did soullessly. "See you are in your own street here it is not safe, we are going to a perfect place now" saying this, he kicked started the bike and they were on the way to where Adnan was desirous to take some friend. Omer did not ask nor was, he listening what Adnan was telling him about the place all he could sense was his world is diminishing, annihilating, compressing and falling within him and in him nothing left alive. The mystery of space vacuums is also defined something like; they are giant holes with such an intense gravity that they even absorb the light. The intensity with which Omer was conscious of (his only conscious that was working, thinking this way) that he has lost, lost all, lost for the life, lost forever, this thinking force was so giant that he had left with no hope alive. The face of his grieved widow mother, the old grandfather of whom, he was the life's only hope, his sitters, their cute children, his brotherly cousins, his benevolent uncle, aunt, the friend all time helpful Ayaz, his home, city country everything lost its meaning just the same as everything falls into those giant holes. No ray of hope of his youth, education, world, career, and life could recover him it was exactly how those giant holes of space swallow the light. He had become a black-hole, falling within. When next time he could listen something said, was Adnan offering him a cigarette and 'why" or "no" were no more in his conscious vocabulary because such concerns are for live brains. He coughed rigorously and two three long smoke strokes baffled his lungs, but he did not quit, as he was not smoking by choice, the same he did not quit with any mind's command of rejection. He had lost control over accepting or rejecting anything. The things were not in his notice but all he could comprehend that there were few more boys in this part of the hall, everybody was smoking, they were laying or half-laying and among two three boys there was an ash tray and they were dusting their fags on it, he could not notice but there was a boy next to him sniffing something from the back of his palm, some boys, after taking one two smokes laying in a deep slumber. Now it was his fag or of another boy and he picked from the ash-tray mistakenly or it was the next to him boy who had made him sniff too, but for last two three smokes his all feelings, consciousness begin to subside, his body was like a running machinery and as if all workers by and by have left, and their machines first slower down than like stopped, or as if his body was being mold in the cult of plaster of pairs drying as dead stiffs, the first thing was his sight getting blur. The green top of billiard table, which was visible from his position in a wall size looking mirror, was now stretching in many shapes in green, but what, he could not comprehend. People going coming here and there were like a big busy fish market. When last time he could hear something, it was a song being played on sound system "sky fall by Adele" and it continued playing for centuries, he had lost sense for time-accuracy after many centuries the same song was on, with horrible effects, what! many centuries ago, yes for him it was like the same, from green of the table top his sight reminded him of something else green and then he could look at his father standing in the paradise, the grass in the paradise was green, then his other family members, then somewhat wakefulness due to loud 'sky fall' moved him to hell where evil spirits were being dragged actually his half shut eyes were seeing a dozing boy was being taken by two boys to the another room, the voice of the song then made him visualize another feast, his Sara laughingly went with another boy but no it was not Sara it was another real girl whom his half shut eyes were looking. The model boy had started deal in dolls and it was a pick-point for them. Omer somehow succeeded in raising his hand as to save Sara from going with another boy it was the mightiest effort of conscious brain which he had made after the set-back. His vision was getting blur and his eyes were half opened but what he could see his mind could not comprehend, the only thing that still working was somewhat his listening, the song which was being played for centuries just muffled its noise then he started listening some kind of humming, the humming sound started clearing but it took another century perhaps. Not only clear but loud also, it became more, more clear, it was not humming but it was some soft recitation of the Holy

Quran, after some time he could discern the voice, that was of his grandfather, perhaps it was paradise, he had seen his father already there. The recitation started smoothing his heartbeat, with the listening of the recitation his mind concentrated on the voice and as soon as the mind could get control over listening his other functions started to come in rhythm the first improvement was seen in pulse, and heart rate, this improved the breathing however he was still not breathing at his own.

When last time Omer's mother saw him, he was watering the plants, seeing him doing this she went upstairs to see the room of the driver, if it was properly done because he was about to stay for another night before leaving for the village, he just went to Faisalabad to leave the small car with that family and to bring with him the big vehicle in order to take the boys and grandfather to the village with computer machines. She was not sure of the bell but a knocking sound, she heard, that was all she could remember, afterwards nobody had seen Omer, Ayaz the first person to ask was also ignorant of Omer's such disappearance. First time in his life Omer bothered not to ask for the permission or even telling. He just had left leaving the door unlocked. Grandfather had been to the laundry shop, two streets back to make the man finish in time. Ayaz was watching TV he was at home and he was completely unaware of Omer's any other program instead both the families were so excited for the village trip, Ayaz, Father, his brothers all started searching for him. They were in search of a person who had least references, least number of people were his acquainted, friends, just one, having no bike which could provide an excuse that bike must have got some problem detaining

him to the workshop, a person who was having no cell-
phone to explain his absence, not even a balance-out,
betray-down cell, the easy it was to get information about
him the difficult it was as the same to search further. All
shops were checked, he had been to none, academy teacher
was also contacted the one who used to come for Omer
and Ayaz, the Stat Teacher, he was unaware of any clue,
all possible class fellows were contacted, Ayaz went to ask
at Adnan's place, they the family of Adnan refused even
to have knowledge about their own son, saying he goes on
hangouts and comes late or sometimes stays with some
friend, they also added in the information that Adnan
had been interested in working in a call center right after
exam so he must have gone there, but the whereabouts of
call center nobody knew, it was a type of a family. Getting
dark someone suggested to report in the police station but
grandfather refused, he was still hopeful. The driver from
Faisalabad had arrived to see this unexpected situation,
grandfather made a casual phone call to Faisalabad to
inform that the driver they sent has reached but he did
not tell nor could he find any clue even if for joke sake
Omer had gone there, but nothing was so. Ayaz mother
was sitting with Omer's mother in Omer's house both the
ladies were praying intensely, the driver suggested; we
must all stay with telephones if he tries to contact. This
suggestion could be their only possible mean before going
to the police station. That same night when the grandfather
resolved to report in the police station, sometimes after
mid-night Ayaz elder brother got to attend a phone call it
was saying "Go see your friend in x hospital" the person on
the phone spoke a name of an expensive private hospital of
a more posh area far from this place. One thing was sure
whosoever phoned knew very well of Ayaz and Omer's

friendship. Not only this he also knew Ayaz number, it was so upsetting for the elder brother but it was not the time to think on these clues so immediately Ayaz his elder brother, grandfather reached to the hospital, there they found somebody has got him admitted, leaving the guardian space unchecked, grandfather and Ayaz both were taken to the emergency, Ayaz elder brother tried to grasp information about the men who brought him here, all he could get to know they were two boys young like Ayaz and they were in a hurry as to catch a flight and they found him on the road and they also used hospital desk phone to a number which turned out to be Ayaz land-line number. Among all speculations only one had a loose end and that was, their excuse of urgency for the air-port which infect was justifying those boys having been responsible, somewhat of Omer's this plight and they made a quick escape, the good part that they informed and paid some of the hospital admitting charges. They were someone knew Ayaz and Omer so they must be from their school. Ayaz elder brother was confused, what to do with those scoundrels without their virtue they could not know of Omer. He wanted very much to pay the money they spent on Omer's admit then to slap them heavily and ask them to stay away from his younger brothers. Ayaz brother was walking to and fro in the corridor of the hospital clenched his fists. The doctor on duty was calming the grandfather because what he was seeing was as if along time kept hold sand grains were losing down from the fist. He collapsed just the same sack like his grandson had. His eyes fixed on Omer whose body was being monitored by various machines, and many lines have gripped his body through finger, on chest and in veins some supply was being transported and on the top an oxygen mask was fit right on his nose. This all was so harassing for the already shed old man that it was hard to make him understand, the doctor and some assistance explained what had happened to him, "It was nothing only he had smoked or inhaled some highly effective drug", while telling this he the doctor kept asking Did he smoke, in response both grandfather and Ayaz almost retaliated in a stern No, the doctors nodded each other and continued, that his body had never experienced any drug so the strong drug smoke effected ever so strongly. It is just the sleep, hardly they had said just the sleep the grandfather agitated "If it was just the sleep then why so many lines are attached to him", sensing the sensitivity of the grandfather's worry the senior doctor putting his hand on Siraj-ud-din's shoulder more politely explained "in such a sleep the brain functions get slower to normal brain system. When we sleep normally, the brain functions get slower in normal sleep too but this sleep is forced to the brain and the brain gets abnormally slow and subsequently all body functions get slower, sometimes it can be dangerous", with the word dangerous grandfather's calming posture again got alert and he looked at the doctor with some alarm, the doctor getting that, compensated saying "But in his case he is out of danger only we want to examine him until he comes out of his deep sleep as natural then we will observe him for half an hour more and then he is discharged, take him home", grandfather's brilliance of eyes were worth seen, he asked to make sure, "Take him home?," "Yes take him home", The doctor replied in same enthusiasm. "And what should we give him for food?" Ayaz made his first question; doctor looked at him asking who he is to the patient, "Am friend", Ayaz spoke, "He is our own child also neighbor, his elder brother has also come", grandfather added, he never forgets anybody's kind deed, doctor smiled and jokingly said "Give juice, soup anything but for next twelve hours do not give solid or spicy just that and then enjoy any food". Grandfather was allowed to sit and watch him awake on his own, and thereupon he started reciting the Holy Quran sitting beside Omer's bed.

Chapter 16

Adnan was playing billiard it was free for him for the night he had introduced a friend just today so there he was on billiard, the environment of the inside has its own theme, nobody bothers other, there were mini-bars, refrigeration, low lights, music rest-rooms there on the smoke corner where he could take glimpse of his friend Omer, was inhaling or smoking some costly brand, Adnan had high ambitions for his friend, recently the model boy, the owner of that place has started Pink-Picks to allow girls so it will be soon a time when he will forget his that girl. Adnan had seen girls coming here were much more stylish and full with beauty enhancing items, so such a place would be a good solution to Omer's grief, he was thinking this when the same academy boy, the middle man who would speak on behalf of the model boy came to him, asking who is the boy he brought today, Adnan told that he is a friend and he will properly join the club today is his first day. "First day umm" his words were mimicked ironically from behind them by the model boy, Adnan had not listened him this way ever so startled by his crude behavior he looked at him, and he, pointed them towards the smoking corner where his friend was lying unconscious, the clumsy position in which he was stretched, was evident that his body had been moved away by dragging his legs awkwardly. Too much for Adnan, ran he to see his friend, Omer was lying unconscious he tried to wake him, he patted him, he also called him but it was something more than sleep, "What happened to him, what happened to my friend" Adnan was getting severe, "He was smoking casual brand", the academy boy came near seeing Omer with fear, ""Had he never smoked" asked he the academy boy, "Never, he is from a very good, noble family" Adnan agitated, "This is not the place for noble chickens, take him away from here", the first true portrait became visible to Adnan of the model, the model of bones and pits. "He needs medication Boss" the academy boy still had heart the big wonder why he worked with that Boss. "He needs garbage box, came here for free luxury, now out you both" Model boy smashing a glass on the floor howled after them. The two managed, Omer in between them on Adnan's bike and their only way was a nearest hospital, though quite expensive but they could not ride the bike in threes in the middle of the night. The hospital however got him admitted in the emergency but the person in charge persistent that the guardians must come so Adnan had to invent the story of catching the flight, and about him, they found on road, but he also phoned Ayaz, careful him he did not use his cell for the phone and then he made escape, Adnan was so afraid of the grind of the events that he did not come that night to his home.

After pulse and improved heart beat, the first visible sign his body made was the movement of his eyeball under his close-lids. This continued with rapid motion and he slightly opened his eyes, it was blurring though but it took another half a minute to settle his focus and now he was capable to see and realize, when suddenly the elder brother of Ayaz asked many questions the doctor asked them do not make him think much let him remember everything itself. He got discharged; at home his mother was told that while driving a bike on rent, he fell, with no apparent injury, and became unconscious. It was already too much for her, and she scolded why he got the bike on rent and why he made suffered all and everyone she was about to beat when grandfather hold Omer, saying, "He is already feared, much feared, he said he is sorry, he said on the way, he just said" while Ayaz mother holding Omer's mother back also said, "We should talk to him we should not beat him see he is already looking so weak, and who knows he hasn't eaten something" this worked effectively and Omer's mother instead of beating went inside. While the elders around Omer asked him to go inside and ask for forgiveness from his mother.

The next day the group was on his way to the village and nobody asked Omer anything, Grandfather had asked everybody to remain quiet and ask nothing as he was sure that he is so embarrassed that he will never do that again. The journey had been very enjoyable; the driver kept playing tracks of their favorite albums. They kept enjoying snakes they carried. The village was some one hour drive ahead from the district shekhupura, they reached well before the lunch-time, and first they went to the NGO office that was adjacent to the school building, initially all that land was of Siraj-ud-din's father. The NGO office building used to be his home and the big courtyard, later he donated for the school building. With the support of local people, and NGO funds some rooms were constructed to shape it a school. It was their first day of arrival so the young teachers, the boys Omer and Ayaz only built repute with the children, who had already gathered in school ground. Afterwards they enjoyed the lunch on the request of office. The classes were about to start early next morning, with enrollment work and with time-division for different groups of children. The young teachers were free for the day so they were taken to the tube-well. They also enjoyed seeing fresh water, Ayaz was more excited, he tried to climb the tree but could not do that so perfectly and another village boy climbed many branches higher to him. The boys were taken to the fields it was rice harvest season and the fields were filled with water. The sunlight reflection through the water was so dazzling,

It was third day only and Sara's hand design of *mehndi* had disappeared, it was strange for Sara's mother, for she was planning to pay a visit with Sara to her own and Rehman's unavoidable but not invited relatives for the news break of Sara's engagement with a UK based maternal cousin moreover that was the best parlor she got the appointment for engagement event. Sara's mother could never imagine that her daughter had been rigorously washing towels in her washroom to erase the mehndi print, she also did not let the boy jimmy to wear her the ring and her mother had to do this as Rehman too did not like this liberal way of ceremony so Rehmans's wife could not force her daughter to wear the ring from the boy. Not only this but with each prayer she would pray only one thing, him. It was difficult for her to let all these things happen, and each time when she would feel helpless she would cry in washroom but never made anybody knew that. What the first thing first she did, were the two possible options, she shut before her, one to accept Jimmy or emmy (anybody) in her life and the second was to commit suicide. She refused to do both and with full clarity of heart and soul she prayed only, and within the same week things processed.

It was so pure, peaceful and polite sitting and watching the sun set that Omer felt much relief, because the travel, the whole day seeing new people or projecting themselves, as something different, as the instructors of computer literacy, that he could not sit by himself. The events of last two days flashed through his memory. He felt deep sorry for his family who suffered for his irresponsible act. He thought about his family his friend and promised to himself that he shall make them happy by becoming more responsible. Then he thought about Adnan who took him there, Adnan reminded him of a saying "A wise enemy is better than a foolish friend", Omer was confused he wanted to show Adnan the right path and he wanted to help him quit smoking but at the same time another saying was much more alarming and that was an intimidation against the bad company. But before the sun set he made his mind to help Adnan to improve and become good. Love is so occupying that all the rest of the thoughts are thought immediately and mind is made cleared and reconcile to think only about love. The last and lasting thought dropped a drop with the dropping sun. He did not want to cry he had to go in and then to the prayer and he had just made promise to make people happy. The next day when he got up, the first thought that gripped him was of her and with that he lost liveliness of a youth. All day he kept busy with the help of NGO office workers in separating different students into different categories. But the initial lesson of starting and shutting-down of a computer with power safety instructions had been taught to the children the very first day. Children were little afraid of using that devise, they were taking that too carefully, this over shyness from computer was the first thing they had to remove and for this purpose the NGO office focal person launched a meeting in which suggestions were made to make children computer friendly. Everybody was giving different suggestions. Omer was lost in the same train of thoughts, thinking her all the time, seeking isolation to think her, undisturbed, he has developed a way, giving others the speaking space to reserve for himself a chance to think of her staying un-interactive while a group conversation is going on. Taking the task happily to go and fetch this thing, that thing instead of making something with the team. Engaging people in conversation willingly giving way to make others win and to him draw away. The grandfather could not see all this immediately and Ayaz was thinking that Omer does not like village life much, so instead of asking he started telling the benefits of that pure air, free of pollution. The coaching task was going perfect, majority of the children had been enabled to use the key-board and mouse, and some could type their names, their parents' names and Pakistan Quaid-i-Azam. On every single achievement they were encouraged to use computer as an incentive. The target was to enable a group of students to teach other new learners to make a cycle of good computer users so such incentives were structured to meet the goal the sooner. Toward normal routine Omer did not let anybody find fault in his work he proved more

a serious teacher than Ayaz, children would take liberties
with Ayaz, sometimes on his face calling the Urdu word
for onion just the similar sound of Ayaz, sometimes they
would hide his file and even in the evening children would
love to defeat Sir Piyaz, in cricket but as soon as they
would see Omer, somewhere, they would shrink to serious
sobers. Omer had changed! No, love had changed Omer.
No lost love had changed Omer, and shall he never be able
to love again. He would laugh sometimes so hysterically
that no one else would join only see him. The life here
was so busier and socially connected Omer or Ayaz had
no idea of that. The classes would start early, then another
just before noon than another in afternoon. Different
groups of children would go to work in fields, in brick
making kilns, in carpet weaving so their possible hours to
study were variable (this pattern was already designed and
being followed in school days by the NGO after the need
assessment of the focal-group of mobilizers), keeping their
computer work record, their daily and weekly assessment
file-work, follow up of absent students and making sure
every students attendance in class in best suitable time to
them, sometime visiting the community to convince them
to keep sending their children, then keeping children
happy and willing to come by short-break games in
which teacher had to participate, then in the evenings,
compulsory sitting in the session of local community as to
discuss their progress, keep them motivating to send the
children and top most to bridge the gap between, them
and biased people. The first thing the grandfather noticed
was his appetite decreased to nothing.

Chapter 17

The same week, it was the flight for the Jimmy Afia and their mother back to UK and they flew, without any phone call without any goodbye visit even without bothering them to see them off at the air-port. This, they got to know through another relative which added the injury, a remotely relative who was not even invited on the event. The whole day more than Rehman, his wife, Sara's mother had been completely surrounded by the worst possible fears, however she kept pacifying her husband but to her something was perplexing her horribly. She could wait hardly of their flight landed in UK she phoned her sister to ask if she had reached safely and many other questions about the infant grandson (his sister's grandson, the child of jimmy's elder brother and the same UK national daughter-in-law). In response her sister was giving least gratitude to her sister's so much concern about the change climate, their eight hours nonstop flight. Saying "It is a routine for us no big deal" when Rehman's wife sensed she is not in an easy mood she started talking about the child and daily routine, suggesting different massages helpful in child's growth about its stomach discussion and much more while on the other side her sister was giving cold shoulder on each of her concern but she continued, she stooped her dignity so low as if she had been peeping in the poopy-dippers of the child. On the other side her sister bluntly said that she will call her back the next day and dropped the call...

Somewhere a call was picked, it was 3 am Omer could not sleep even for a single moment the whole night. He had become so helpless, earlier when he would think of her, his eyes would see dreams of someday come true in future, only he needed to make himself capable enough to deserve her and all his labor done in studies would sweetened with this idea. Thinking her now, was bleak, just recollecting the past which could not be revised except in memories and there he could see nothing for the future and such a dead end thinking her, had made him feverish, his mind had become so exhausted of thinking her and same exceeded thinking had taken his sleep away. It was more than the drug inhalation, it was sucking his soul. Recollecting her in all past recollections, seeing her waiting for him, the visit to her home and the two boats together, each moment many, many times he had left but with the images of memories, his tears wet the pillow that night. A humming sound again but not, it was clear, from far off, the *fajer* prayer call, the *azan*. Already had been up, made his way to the mosque. He was the first who entered the mosque. The light was just one dimly but enough for ablution and prayer. Here sitting alone and doing ablution with cold underground water pumped through the hand-pump, he reminded one similar evening, he was in the unfinished mosque, it was early winter and water was same cold and there, on the floor he offered prayer and did dua for the safe and secure stay of Sara in her father's home until he comes for her hand, it was when he did not know even her name, it was then when she was not yet, proved a good girl with no valentine friend, it was then when he had not called her, by her name, it was then when he had not heard his name from her, it was when, he had not visited her house, it was before then when his fingers were only some beads away from her fingers, it was before then when their boats stopped together next to each other and it was then when she visited his home and befriended everyone. Thinking this startled him, while he was praying one evening so desperately for her safety and for her hand to be in his, forever, in a right full way he did not pray for these other things the miracle that his grandfather turned out to be her father's best acquainted, their visit to each other and then so many other things he could not even think and they happened. He had been so blind and could not see this much, his Allah kept giving him to keep him satisfied, happy and grateful. Thus bending situations all in their favor first by making both the family elders, the decision-makers friends of each other and thus drawing them close, He the Lord have his plans best known to Him. We are creatures and we must always pray for His benevolence, he went to do ablution again because a hard-core pray had made him moan. This time he had shed his last tear. The prayer in congregation, then the recitation of the Holy Quran until dawn made him feel much light. The following day, however was spent lazily he wanted to sleep, but there was no situation.

Zakaullah the Zaki Sara's elder brother, Rehman's only son who had been to Australia for last many months, rushed straight from the air-port to the hospital, there in the ICU his mother was admitted. It was about ten in the night, his father and sister both were already there, and on approaching near them he realized how much his family needed him at this time of chaos. Not only his sister let her control loose on tears but his father broke like a child, trembling and couldn't been supported even in his sons arms, falling, collapsing almost, this horrified the son God forbidden, if the worst has happened and he is late…, he made his father sit, first on a seat of hospital corridor, Sara forgetting tears horrified as the same to see his dauntless father shattering this way, brought water. The three were sitting closer, the three were quiet as the Zaki knew on what news her mother got that sudden heart attack but he did not want to discuss things just then as Sara was also there, after sitting brief with his family meanwhile caressing his father's shoulders he made a move asking Sara to take care of father and went to discuss with the doctor on duty about his mother's case. After having some discussion with the doctor on duty and seeking the senior doctor's opinion he came to his father telling him that the crucial moment has over but since the heart rate has to be monitored so it will take another couple of days monitoring her. It was time now to allow the visitors to see the patient, but they were strictly asked to stay brief and quiet. All three wore gowns and made their visit one after another under the supervision of the duty nurse. They could only see their mother who was attached with so many lines and so many different sized monitors, those were reading her blood, heart, and pulse and breathing course. After they had been out Zaki took them to the hospital canteen to give them a relief and to have some time together. Upon sitting there he tried to distract their arrested nerves by telling how difficult it had been to catch a flight with least stops and he came via Abu Dhabi availing one stop while some other flights were making their stops at Singapore, Bangkok, and Kuala Lumpur. He also told Sara that he has brought rare sets of artificial jewelry for her, after relaxing them a little he brought something from the canteen which the three ate without eager, then he asked Sara to take father home and let him sleep, and Zaki also suggested her to sleep as they had been here for last two days. Then escorting them to the parking and giving instructions to the driver to whom he had already called sensing his father must not be asked to drive, also put his luggage in the car tail thus sent them home talking soft things about Melbourne, he also assured Sara who was disturbed with the idea that his brother had been on travel and he needs the rest most, on this he laughed and told her that the work and study load has made him a tough guy and he is habitual of wake full nights, and he had been sleeping in the plane and finally he assured his father that one of his friend is willing to come and stay with him all the time so they must not worry. Finally to give them a happy move asked his sister to keep the *biryani* ready for him when he comes home or else forget about the jewelry, she laughed, this he all needed, now he could stay up all night untiring. Zakaullah has changed; one could never imagine of him so warmly loving and friendly to her younger sister or is it typically a tradition of eastern families that the closest male figures stay poised and detached somehow but one thing was true 'Still waters run deep'. It is a quote from a short story The Little Willow by Frances Towers.

Chapter 18

It had been a fortnight since they had arrived in the village. So far almost all the children had become capable of plugging the systems on and shutting them down along with typing their names and some more words in English, they had learned in their formal studies. More children were interested in the work of art and coloring; this improved their mouse hold practice. Grandfather was very happy seeing the young operators busy on machines, it was a like a dream come true, while talking to the focal person of the NGO on the same day, he expressed his wish to arrange a program in which children are encouraged to perform their favorite poems, and their work of art and typing must be displayed in the audience for their applause. The last request the grandfather made, that in next week they want to go back to the city donating the systems to the village school children, they brought to them. This news whereas was a happy one to have the computer systems all for the school children but their leaving, just in the next week fell heavily. Their presence brought a fresh friendly air from the city with the massage of brotherhood; oneness and mutual-growth "I shall not tell the children, these village people attach themselves so strongly you have to tell this news yourself" the focal person from the NGO refused a request of Siraj-ud-din for the first time. "Alright I will tell, not only this but I will also tell them that the next year we will come again with more computers, more instructors so how is that?" Siraj-ud-din smiled he always had some surprise in stock for others. This made the NGO focal person a lot happier; the next project he discussed in a general meeting, upon there it was considered that the next assignment is to master them over the usage of short-keys. Some eleven children were selected through a series of assessment to put them to learn usage of short keys. While the meeting was going on the grandfather got something reminded of and he asked the boys to help the NGO workers search that. These were summer holidays and the teachers of their formal education system were on leave so the drawers of their teaching material were locked. A request was made from the searching members to use master-keys and let the drawers also be searched the request was carried and the drawers were opened. There under the pile of books, study-aids at the bottom, they found, these were the illustrated books of Urdu poems of Allama Muhammad Iqbal, Molana Hali and Ismail Meerthi Nazeer Akber Abadi. They had never been opened, never been bothered to look at to. The history of these books was some two years back Siraj-ud-din collected all long lost poems of easy Urdu, meant for children to make moral lessons easy in rhymes, which had been omitted from the syllabus for reason un known, he compiled them in book-form and after giving good illustration for children's interest thus spending so much money all by himself had sent the packs to various schools, along with this school too but these books were not taught or given to the children. The focal person was not asked for the reason however Siraj-ud-din decided to distribute the books himself on the program that was to be organized after few days.

It took another five days when the hospital discharged Sara's mother. At home she was not allowed to move much frequently and more bed rest was recommended with light food and no stress. Zakaullah was demanding every bit of the detail that happened in his absence, how his aunt the sister to her mother proposed for Sara, how and why in such an instant the engagement was announced and celebrated, his father Rehman was telling him everything in mild version. On the name of Jimmy Zakaullah burst out saying that, that boy has no manners at all to talk to elders whenever someone talks to him instead of paying proper attention he replies while reading sms or mails on his cell phone, he is so arrogant and rude, he also cursed himself on not being here or else such a thing, he would never let happen. He also collected information from the maid and according to her account his mother was on the phone and nobody was around she was crying and saying if we had committed some mistake forgive us but do not break this engagement, we will get ruined, the more the maid could not tell as Zakaullah had closed his eyes pressing his lips, after a pause he managed to speak then he asked how, how did she get that attack, the maid who was already shrunk seeing Zakaullah's facial expressions briefly told that after the phone was dismissed his mother saying abruptly "They have broken, they have broken the engagement" and got fainted holding her chest as if to refrain a severe pain. Zakaullah could not stand anymore and left the place, a crashing sound was heard from where he went.

Chapter 19

The preparations of the program were on full swing, children practiced their favorite poems, skits, mimicries and presented them in such a robust style that one needs to think if someone gets time for the whole life to devote; these children were worth for that. The day came the school ground was swarming with parents, elderly people infants and other children. The session started with the recitation from the Holy Quran and *naat*. The participant came one by one in an organized way to perform his, her best and received the applause. The faculty wing of the NGO had trained the children to face the audience so they were not shy as was presumed, and they had been performing on other platforms before this. After that both the teachers Omer and Ayaz made the audience watch the display of print out of the children's work which met with the huge applause that was meant for the instructors. The NGO focal person also announced that their work shall remain displayed in the office for a record of their achievement. The elders of the village also presented their cordial thanks for the time, and contribution, the city people made, out of their over possessed life, some got too emotional in their deliverance of thanks that one actually wants to stay with them for the life. The session ended with Siraj-ud-din's acknowledgement of NGO and local community's co-operation without which this day could not be achieved. His announcement of the next-year plan was received with thunderous applause. He also distributed the illustrated books of poem collection to each child asking them to read those poems and when next year he would come he would like to listen from them. The session ended perfectly on time as it started raining heavily, people dispersed to check if any leakage might damage their roofs. Grandfather came to the *pikora*-selling person and bought all his freshly fried *pikoras* and distributed to the children, asking the seller to go and enjoy the rain, where else the poor man might go. So sitting right there under the shade of his shop with Siraj-ud-din he started discussing change in life styles. The rain stopped in an hour but it was still cloudy and windy, the village was looking awesomely beautiful.

Rehman had to give more time and attention to his son than to his wife. He knew his son is young and extremely angry so it was important to pacify him first. Rehman was persuading Zakaullah to go back to Australia as his wife's condition was improving, Sara would take her mother out for a short walk in the lawn as was prescribed, she was in a state of dread she never wanted things happen this way, she never wanted her mother got a social humiliation and so seriously ill. This flow of change was undesirable, never on the cost of her mother's life or family repute. Each time when a phone call was to attend she would avoid, asking maid to attend, the show of concern false or true from the family was shattering her whole self. Sensitive daughter taking herself blameworthy for all that, felt guilty and grieved. That night, after coming home from the hospital when her brother arrived right from Australia and sent them home, she making sure her father has gone to sleep, she went to her room and prayed hard. This time only for her mother, for her mother's life, for her family and family's good, she wanted nothing now, she has made harmony with the events, pleading good for the family, realizing that her own good lies in the family good; in each prayer she prayed the same. His thoughts, were nowhere on her mind, but there was quietness and serenity in her heart if not him. The atmosphere of the house had filled with anger, seriousness and silence, the servant party was quieter than the family members, most of the phones were received by the maid and were apologized that she is asleep and thanks for calling, I will inform.

On a sabotage scene, though the dreadful silence prevails after the major destruction yet, some shelling keep disrupting that mournful peace. Zakaullah was sitting in the lawn with his father. Rehman was persuading him softly that he should go back as his mother's condition is improved, then suddenly a phone on Rehman's cell intervened, Rehman, seeing the number did not want to attend but Zakaullah persisted to attend the phone, not only this he also put the louder on and gave that to his father. From the other end some relative, left behind in the old vicinity first asked about his wife, then humiliatingly said that they, (the calling person's family) is seriously concerned lest his daughter should have taken poison just like her paternal aunt, he was enforcing this with the reason that the broken engagement and sudden heart attack of her mother must have smashed her thoroughly. Then he spoke almost two pages of the un-certainty of the living-abroad relatives, loyalty of in-land relatives, subliminally complaining of his opinion was never asked in making that relation, and being avoided, poor fate of daughters and Rehman's the poorest one, having set-backs each time earlier for his sister now for his daughter then concluding sadly that had she been died like her aunt it would have been lot better now who will ask for her hand when her closest relative broke the engagement and he can do *dua* only. The phone ended Zakaullah took the handset from his father who was still with a down casted head. Zakaullah too was sitting quiet for that was over too much to his level of tolerance. It took quiet a time to enable him talk sensibly

"Papa is that all, the bad asset we have earned so far? See in business we are next to none *Alhamdulsillah*! But why in social life we are so bankrupt of well-wishers, we did not deserve that"

Rehman spoke sadly "It is how the world works people keep lashing you keep pricking you yet there are few people still in the world who encourage others, who are happy truly on other's happiness and it is not so there are good people too"

Zakaullah had to remain quiet for a while as he did not want to discuss this unexperienced optimism then he spoke "I want that Sara should proceed her studies and no more engagement at least when I am not here",

His father smiled patting his shoulder said "Do not worry nothing like this in your absence but one thing is important, what I see in the world the sooner the daughters get settled the better it is, see your mother, and I am not strong enough" on this Zakaullah hold his father's hand nodding as if that his father must not think weak, "you had seen me that night..." Rehman's voice texture changed, "and our relatives" he continued, "you know that all, so in such circumstances we may not delay much. Since you are not here, yesterday your mother was saying that, she wants that, it is always blamed to the girl on such breakage of engagements, the sooner she will be engaged the better it would be"

Thinking his father was right Zakaullah asked "Don't you know good nice people out of the family you have big business circle?"

this question put Rehman in serious thoughts, "Alright let your mother get alright then we shall be able to do something", saying this he got up went inside but turned in the middle of the way and called louder to his son as if some good thought has crossed his mind, "Today I will take you to the mosque it is new at the end of the street",

"I have offered prayer there yes it is good" Zakaullah answered in the same calling voice,

"That is a nice man, good nice family" it was that or something like that his father's voice had regained same usual energy. Zakaullah could not understand what his father was talking about because he was talking about the mosque first, but he did not go in to ask father, sitting in the cloudy, windy morning in the lawn chair, it was so relaxing, he closed his eyes and from nowhere a feeling occurred to him as if there will be no problem left anymore and things will automatically, be alright...

Chapter 20

It had not been an hour sitting under the shed of the *pikora*-seller's shop talking with him on the technology that has hit village life and its influence over the villagers when suddenly Siraj-ud-din' caught the sight of something from behind the pikora seller. There had become a small pool of rain-accumulated water and while focusing pikora-seller some quivering object at that pool diverted Siraj-ud-din's attention, now, what was that, it was something white, and it was floating nearer then he could see that clear, it was a paper boat floating with frequent stops, it would quiver a bit with the gush of wind, it was no more floating now, probably it was struck in some stone. The sight of that boat put Siraj-ud-din in amaze as there was no work done in papers that day. At school children used to be given papers only when a task is assigned, they were never given home-take study material and most importantly there was no child around, all had left. Siraj-ud-din now became curious to know the boat and more about the sailor. He stood from his seat standing straight as if to straightening his limbs he stretched; going to the other end of the shed he spotted the sailor. There was a boy in T-shirt trousers sitting on the ground just by the pool embracing his knees bending his head on his knees looking still in the quivering of the water, but his looks were not pursuing the boat. Had he been closer and had stood longer by that boy he could also observe that, it was not just the boat but the boy has deposited his earning of grief to the mother nature, a single tear slipped down from his eye and mingled with the rain water thus inseparably. The boy was calm; he wasn't looking to the boat, as if he had become aloof of the boat's float or boat's fate. Some nights before what he realized of miracle one after another seemed to him a dream in the life or life in the dream, Perhaps he had surrendered. This would be the last installment which he had paid. Her thoughts were nowhere on his mind, yes there was quietness and serenity in his heart if not her.

Turning to the pikora-seller Siraj-ud-din asked for his permission to leave and carefully made his way from the other end of the shed walking towards the mosque however there was still much time in the *dhuhr* prayer he kept on thinking. Some images of real events flickered through his mind, another such boat tugged in the vipers of the wind-screen then the same boat, he had noticed on Omer's study table throughout the exam. There was some connection and he had no doubt about it, one column of his formation was still oblique, why Omer drugged him so much, by now he has reached the mosque. Entered he in, sitting on the prayer mat resting his back with the wall, the cross ventilation of the mosque had cooled the inner atmosphere it was so relaxing, he reinstated his calculation about his grandson, his recent observation about Omer, his lost appetite, quietness, and finding always a place away from others is a subsequent effect not of the drug but the drug itself was a strong reaction against something, something missing and that someone can be none other than a Love, Siraj-ud-din though has grown old but the state of being in love has not lost from his memories. He also realized that these later effects are however slower but infect swallowing his soul more than an instant drug. Whoever Omer is missing but Omer is sad because of staying away from someone... What! His grandson was in love! This gave him a start he stood up suddenly his soul lightened as if all the riddles have solved. Visualizing again all events gave a hearty laugh because the chain of events solved another puzzle that, that girl very sweet, her name was ...Sara yes Sara Rehman's daughter also loves his grandson. Many days ago a boat in the vipers seemed to him the sweetest thing, Sara resounded in his mind as the sweetest name and he was now walking to and fro convincing himself "Yes there is no wonder after all they were in the same school, they are of the same age and what else is required for a perfect love" the more he would think the better he became clear with the idea that his by nature shy grandson and that a modest girl from a decent family can do no further then leaving paper boats in reciprocation and it is his task to join the two souls together. He wanted to play in that challenge. It was a reinvigorating project. Walking up and down in the mosque courtyard he was thinking and on each thought he was smiling. Things appeared to him, were not so difficult. Rehman already had a high opinion about his family so all he needed was to initiate in the name of Allah this thought relaxed him and Siraj-ud-din sat down again on the prayer mat resting his head with the wall he was doing a silent pray. He closed his eyes and from nowhere a feeling occurred to him as if there will be no problem left anymore and things will automatically, be alright... after some time he made a phone call to his son in Faisalabad for detailed instructions then waited for some time then received a call from the same son from Faisalabad about the instructions that were being carried out. By that time it was Dhuhr, Ayaz and Omer were entering in the mosque with some village folks, the prayer was offered, he asked them to pack the bags and stay ready for they are going to make the move early in the morning. The boys could not understand this sudden change in the plan according to the last discussion they were told that another whole day will be for them to enjoy leisure in the village. Taking the rest of few hours of that day for granted, they met with their new friends and said them good bye, right after the Fajr Prayer they were on their way back. On the way they got to know that the driver did not come straight, alone, from Faisalabad but also brought Omer's uncle and aunt. First he dropped them in Omer's house in Lahore then he reached to the village last night, and before dawn they all were towards home. Omer could not notice why grandfather frequently looks at him with a peculiar smile and why he asked the driver to replay a track "asi gabru Punjabi dil jide naal laiyan yaarian" Things were difficult, why his uncle and aunt came so unexpected from Faisalabad, why dada g decided to go back earlier, but Omer's mind would not bother him any more to think of whys. A dull mind gets sharpen in love but what happens to a sharp mind, and when the love surrenders, somebody should think this over...

The last chapter

The recently appointed *Molvi* of that newly constructed mosque was pleased to see both father and son together, telling that he has seen this young man (Zakaullah) in the mosque already but he did not know he was Rehman's son. Rehman told about his son been to Australia then he asked about Siraj-ud-din, he had not seen him for many days. On this that *Molvi* was surprised, telling "What a co incidence the same Siraj-ud-din had phoned me in the evening asking about you", and he also told that Siraj-ud-din had ben to village and he would come tomorrow morning. It was pleasant news however Rehman had completely forgotten his plan to the village with the grandson. The conversation summed up with a message from Siraj-ud-din that, he wanted to pay a visit the next day, on some personal account, and if Rehman has some time for that. On this Rehman was very happy and told that he is also looking forward to see him, taking his son back to home; Rehman enjoyed an electrifying energy to tell all about Siraj-ud-din his newly made friend.

Only two men, Grandfather and his son from Faisalabad went to Rehman's house in the morning and expressed solemnly yet gracefully, the purpose of their meeting. The two were Siraj-ud-din and his son, they were received very cordially. It was too unexpected for this father and the son. Only yesterday they were thinking to get themselves acquainted with good people outside the family. Rehman was proud how decently they put forth their proposal, his son Zakaullah had never come across to so simple, nice and true people. The way both grandfather and son the uncle to Omer asked for Sara that was so respectful that Zakaullah could allow them to marry with his sister right away. During the previous night discussion Zakaullah and Rehman had been convinced that, the man Siraj-ud-din and his family is nice people but having this interaction this solemn way of asking somebody's daughter and when such a tragedy had fallen over them with a broken engagement social embarrassment and mother's serious condition on the top. But this visit of these people affirm them of Allah's blessings in recent series of events no matter shocked they had been. It was too good far too over their imagination; after expressing their wish for becoming one family, they requested to allow their family women to meet the daughter and her mother of their house and nothing more on any given Sunday.

Then for some more years they were made disallowed to see each other, they were extremely happy on the decision elders took for them. Sara got admission in the college and Omer also took admission with more studious efforts for the career as he was to merry Sara as soon as he could come up to a career. For them there was still time but the quick change that took place, that very day, was that, Rehman brought out his younger sister's photo folding frame of twin photos from Sara's room and placed it in full open view in his own room, he could forgive his sister now, and to his own daughter Sara he started missing even before her getting away with her husband. Sara's mother took little time to realize that through black mailing and threats marriages are not made. The girl, whom once Omer's mother hold by the arm, now was about be her right hand forever. Omer's sisters would lovingly remind their innocent would-be sister-in-law of how she was struck on the road, as for the children until Sara will get married to Omer and would come finally to the house then these same children will do their home-work under her supervision because she will remain their favorite Sara aunt. Adnan and the middle-man boy from Adnan's academy took time to improve their ways; Omer returned the amount Adnan had spent on his hospitalization through his first intern ship pay, until then Adnan had become good, the same evening he visited Omer with a gift of neck-tie, he knew the money he spent on Omer was his atonement for what he did to him, he had become a frequent guest just like Ayaz. Ayaz had still time to marry so he managed to go abroad for higher studies on his scholarship sponsors, after his A-levels. Once when Sara and Omer would get married, they would recall the days of their early love as a phase of the most loving one, in love. Many have loved but love wins only when Allah wills.

Glossary

Alhumdulilah Arabic expression of praising Allah in order to thanks Allah

Azan is a call for prayer or salat.

Biryani is a popular dish of rice and roasted meat rich in flavors and spices.

Bukhari or Ṣaḥīḥ al-Bukhārī (Arabic: صحيح البخاري), is one of the Kutub al-Sittah (six major hadith collections) of Sunni Islam. These Prophetic traditions, or hadith, were collected by the Persian Muslim scholar Muhammad al-Bukhari, after being transmitted orally for generations. In some circles, it is considered the most authentic book after the Quran. The Arabic word sahih translates as *authentic* or *correct*. **Muslim** is also a collection of Hadith.

Dada g Dada is a word for the grandfather and g is an expression for yes please. Here it is for the respect of grandfather.

Deevan-i-Ghalib is a poetic collection of the famous poet of the sub-continent; Mirza Asadullah Baig Khan Ghalib. He was an Urdu and Persian poet during the last years of the Mughal Empire.

Dua is the same heart-core prayer. Muslims can do dua at any time anywhere. Raising both their hands (palms skywards) joining the palms in a cup shape (or separate) as if for begging from Allah for His blessings

Dupta is 2by3 meter cloth of muslin to cover head shoulders and torso, an essential of Pakistani women's wear

Durse means a session of lecture particularly for preaching Islam and its commandments.

Eid is a day of festivity and joy for the Muslims. It is celebrated after the month of Ramadhan

Gulab-jamun is a brown soft juicy ball made out of fine flour, eggs, dry milk when fried, dipped in the sweetened thick liquid a popular item of Pakistani sweet-meat.

Hafeez Center a shopping plaza in Lahore (gulberg area), it is a market particularly for the computer systems, and lap tops, mobile phones and accessories sale and repair.

Hulwa is a soft sweet dish made of semolina or crushed carrots or chick-peas. It is made in cooking oil or ghee or butter.

Imam Sahib Imam who leads and Sahib is a respected word. Imam is a person who leads in the prayer standing ahead of the rest, usually such a person is a qualified religious scholar deployed in the mosque by the local government.

Kebab is made of minced meat, boiled and ground in spices then the palm-size tablet shape is given and lastly fried in a flat pan in very less oil often served for snakes with tea.

Mamu a relation a word for mother's brother.

Mehndi or henna is a paste of thoroughly ground leaves of a plant. Girls apply that paste on palms on eid or on marriage functions for some time then it leaves a reddish-brown color, it is also applied on hair for conditioning it has very good smell too. Now chemicals are mixed in the mehndi for more lasting color effects.

Molvi Another word for Imam, he also gives (azan) the call for prayer salat.

Naat is a poem written or read in the praise of the last prophet Muhammad (peace be upon him)

Nikkah is a legal marital contract in Islam and the couple can be parted only through divorce.

Pikora is made of chick-peas; simmer in spices onion or potato deep fried and served, with or without tea, with tomato or tamarind catch-up. It is enjoyed most on rainy season

Poori-chunny a poori is a very thin roti of fine-flour deep-fried and chunny is the pulses cooked with chicken and species often served with sooji hulwa the sweet dish made of semolina. It is a famous breakfast dish in Pakistan particularly of Lahore it is always bought from the shops in the morning or is eaten there upon in the shops (shopkeepers do arrange seating arrangements) to enjoy the hot aromatic breakfast.

Roti is made of wheat and an essential food item of Pakistani food

Tandoor a shop where roties are cooked

Ucha ucha if spoken once means good but if spoken twice and together that means alright, I understand.

Urdu Bazar (bazar means market) a famous market in Lahore for all kinds of books and stationary. Publishers, printing offices and dealers in books have offices there.

Zind-a-bad a word for Bravo

There are five prayers obligatory in a day in Islam,

Fajr (pre-dawn) Fajr begins at subh saadiq - true dawn or morning twilight when the morning light appears across the full width of the sky and ends at sunrise

Dhuhr (midday) The Dhuhr prayer starts after the sun passes its <u>zenith</u>, and lasts until Asr

Asr (afternoon) The Asr prayer starts when the shadow of an object is the same length as the object itself (or, according to <u>Hanafi</u> fiqh, twice its length) and lasts till sunset. Asr can be split into two sections; the preferred time is before the sun starts to turn orange, while the time of necessity is from when the sun turns orange until sunset.

Maghrib (sunset) The Maghrib prayer begins when the sun sets, and lasts till the red light has left the sky in the west.

Isha'a (night The Isha'a prayer starts when the red light is gone from the western sky, and lasts until the rise of the "white light" (fajar sadiq) in the east. The preferred time for Isha'a is before midnight, meaning halfway between sunset and sunrise.

Jumma means Friday but usually it is referred to the Friday prayer that replaces the dhuhr prayer performed on the other six days of the week. The precise time for this congregational prayer varies with the mosque, but in all cases it must be performed after the dhuhr and before the asr times. If one is unable to join the congregation, then they must pray the dhuhr prayer instead. This salat is compulsory to be done with ja'maat for men. Women have the option to perform Jumm'ah in the mosque or to pray dhuhr